William James Dawson

A Vision of Souls with Other Ballads and Poems

William James Dawson

A Vision of Souls with Other Ballads and Poems

ISBN/EAN: 9783744787871

Printed in Europe, USA, Canada, Australia, Japan

Cover: Foto ©Andreas Hilbeck / pixelio.de

More available books at **www.hansebooks.com**

A VISION OF SOULS,

WITH OTHER BALLADS AND POEMS.

A VISION OF SOULS,

WITH OTHER BALLADS AND POEMS.

BY

W. J. DAWSON.

LONDON:

ELLIOT STOCK, 62, PATERNOSTER ROW, E.C

1884.

CONTENTS.

A BOOK OF DAYS.

ERRATA.

Page 41, line 2 from bottom, for *buds* read *beds*.

Page 97, line 13 from top, for *plans* read *plan*.

A VISION OF SOULS.

I.

THE COMING OF THE SOUL.

IN God's hands lie the souls of men,
 At God's feet spreads the infinite,
Filled with its wheeling worlds, as when
 He made the earth and made the light.
And like a dove of white each soul
 Flies forth across the abysmal sea,
Where golden suns and systems roll,
 To find the life that is to be.

The myriad millions of the just,
 The seraphim, in fiery rings
Bow down, and every world of dust
 Is brightened with the flash of wings.

And when each soul flies forth from them,
   Through deeps of gloom, and seas of light,
A music, as of Bethlehem,
   Floats forth, and floods the hollow night.

Thy crystal gates of light unbar,
   A holy silence fills the sky:
New waves of splendour from each star
   Break at the feet of God, and die.
And far in some dark world of His,
   Half-circled in its light and gloom,
A mother shares God's awful bliss:
   Her child has quickened in the womb.

And evermore before God's face,
   Like snow within a driving wind,
There move the souls white-clothed in grace,
   Whose earthly pain is left behind.
And evermore from God's right-hand ·
   New souls fly forth, like sparks of light
From clear white fires by whirlwinds fanned,
   And fall into the outer night.

And through the roar of winds and earths
   Forever circling round His throne,
And through ten thousand splendid births
   Of day and night, zone after zone;

A Vision of Souls.

Through wastes of light and dread abyss,
   There floats the newborn infant's cry,
And thus the furthest world of His
   Makes gladder yet the inmost sky.

And angels bearing frankincense
   Of holy thoughts, and myrrh of pain,
And kingly gifts, prefiguring whence
   The soul arose, fly forth ; and twain
Stand at the lowly mother's head,
   And twain about her feet, that they
From silent censers twain may shed
   A sunlight gathered from God's day.

In God's hands lie the souls of men,
   Like doves that crowd within a nest ;
At God's knees throng in order then
   The myriad millions of the blest ;
And all the worlds in rings of light
   Burn on their way about His feet ;
And He creates as seems Him right,
   And calls to death, when death is meet.

II.

THE SOUL'S GROWTH.

THE holy soul hath found its place,
   The little heart of life begins;
A silent bud-like human face
   Sleeps stainless in a world of sins.
The little hands are claspt together,
   The lips are shut, the child sleeps well,
Like fairy found in azure weather
   Asleep within a lily's bell.

And in the child's eyes lingers yet
   A gentle light fallen from God's throne,
Like sunlight when the sun has set,
   Like twilight when the day is gone.
And in the child's heart there is heard
   Heaven's music, but no breath of wrong;
The chords of sense are faintly stirred
   By gently dying winds of song.

And on the child-soul there is felt
   The warm touch of God's shaping hand;
The yesterday, where myriads knelt
   And waited for the Lord's command;

The memory of a world that was
  More clear than sense of one begun,
A sea of souls, a sea of glass,
  And God's face shining like a sun.

High on the trembling bridge of air,
  Stretched like a gossamer's gold thread
Between the earth and God, the fair
  White angels move with noiseless tread.
And all day long they go and come,
  And whisper round the growing soul
The language of its former home,
  Lest it forget its future goal.

And silently the soul displays
  Its petals, like a holy flower,
Within whose golden womb the rays
  Of day strike wider hour by hour.
And thus it passes from eclipse,
  And feels, but cannot understand
The sweetness of a mother's lips,
  The gentle touches of her hand.

Faint tremblings of intelligence,
  Thrill from the outer world of strife
Along the tightening threads of sense,
  And shake the fragile web of life.

And from the mist kind human eyes,
  Like stars of love, a moment gleam ;
While far away earth's battle-cries
  Sound like a sea heard in a dream.

Then memories of the throne of God
  Die out, and perish one by one ;
The daisy springing from the sod,
  The golden shining of the sun,
The wonder of the starlit arch,
  ' The piping bird, the north wind wild—
Life in its great processional march
  Absorbs the wonder of the child.

The stillness of the summer wood,
  The anger of the winter's night,
The lark's song, pass into the blood,
  Absorbed, as flowers absorb the light.
All sounds and sights, all deed and speech
  Beat round the heart, as waves whose shock
Mark ripples on the sandy beach
  Which soon will be the living rock.

At last into the soul's dim choir
  The singers crowd, all passions come :
Desire, with deep-set eyes of fire ;
  And Daring, with his brows of doom ;

A Vision of Souls.

And Hope, whose thrilling linnet note
  Rings through the clouded roof; and Lust,
With snakes of gold wound round her throat,
  And snakes within her heart of dust.

Faint in sealed chambers of the heart
  The secret music's saintly swell
Yet rises; but from street and mart
  Life's trumpets blow, for powers of hell
Are grappling, and the hour has come;
  And with the morrow's dawn, the brave
Young soul shall face the field of doom
  That stretches to the distant grave.

Far on the bridge of gossamer,
  That glimmers like a golden thread
Between the stars, God's hosts appear
  And bless the sleeper in his bed.
And slowly in the blood-red east
  The wounded day awakes with pain;
Life's tragedy, for best and least,
  Before God's eyes is played again.

III.

THE SOUL'S SINNING.

As in a vision faint yet clear,
　　The dream of sin surroundeth me :
Enchanted woods with leaves all sere
　　Stand knee-deep in a magic sea;
And winding ways, built up and spanned
　　By golden flowers, run here, run there ;
And fire leaps in the yellow sand,
　　And every footprint is a snare.
　　　　Ah, misery !

No sun shines on the magic sea,
　　The swooning air is warm and gray :
No winds blow, and no storms there be
　　To break the immemorial day.
No lark soars in the heavy sky,
　　And all sounds faint ; and on the shore
No ripple runs : all silently
　　The misty sea flows evermore.
　　　　Ah, misery !

And through the glimmering trees there gleam
   Faint faces, lit with languorous eyes,
That live within a tangled dream
   Too deep for struggle or surprise.
And passionate whispers thrill the calm,
   And wafts of music, as it were
Of feasters bowered in groves of palm,
   Who sing in trance, but do not stir.
       Ah, misery !

A leprosy is on the trees,
   The air is tainted with the tomb ;
The golden flowers are full of bees
   That build a poisonous honeycomb.
The crimson grasses burn the feet,
   And vipers round each knotted bole
Twine like a glittering thread, and meet
   With dreadful eyes the wandering soul.
       Ah, misery !

And in the deep lush grass there stands
   A naked Phantom, on whose breasts
Strong men have died; whose moist loose hands
   Have filled the prisons of hell with guests ;

Whose face is double—one way turned,
　　An angel's drawn to wickedness ;
The other, scarred, and bruised, and burned,
　　A dead face, steeped in hideousness.
　　　　Ah, misery !

"Come back, young soul !"   He will not hear;
　　He leaps into the Phantom's arms !
His mouth is at her mouth of fear,
　　She holds him in her evil charms.
He shall not feel the fire and pain ;
　　As one who sleeps, and turns in sleep
To seek the adulteress yet again,
　　So shall he dream, and shall not weep.
　　　　Ah, misery !

Yea, he shall feel the fire, the pain,
　　Not yet.   The festering rust of shame
Eats slowly through the golden chain,
　　And blisters all the flesh like flame.
Not yet : the Phantom's passionate mouth
　　Is full of honey, and her bosom
Sweet as a flower-bed in the south,
　　Where vestal violets blow and blossom
　　　　Ah, misery !

And all the wood rings with her song,
   And her lithe naked limbs flash forth
Like dancing fire ; and she is strong
   As winds that sweep the frozen north.
O Soul ! that God should make thee fair,
   And save thy sweet child-life for this !
Look at thy temptress : in her hair
   What snakes uncoil ! what adders hiss !
     Ah, misery !

IV.

THE SOUL'S WAKING.

SILENT within the web of sin
   The Soul sits like a drunkard bowed
In shame, with daylight looking in
   Out of an angry thunder-cloud.
Each broken chord of memory makes
   A moaning music, and each thread
Of consciousness in terror shakes,
   As touched by fingers of the dead.
And where is God gone? Is He dead
   Or is He the only one who wakes ?

The Soul ariseth, gathering up
    Her soiled white raiment from the mire,
Like a pale Magdalen, whose cup
    Is drained in bitterness and desire.
With fair feet stained and body scarred
    With wine-red finger-marks of shame,
And brow pain-crowned, and visage marred,
    She stands as one whom all defame.
And where is God gone ?   Is He dead ?
    Or points He too with hand of flame ?

Weeping beside the gates of hell
    The Soul stands pale, and sees within
The moving darkness, like a well
    Of flame, uprise the woe of sin.
And black wings fill the lonely air,
    And cries of spirits in wrath and pain.
Shall the base thing again be fair ?
    Shall the fire burn, but burn in vain ?
And where is God gone ?   Is He dead ?
    Or will He yet shine forth again ?

Yet not within the gates of hell
    The Soul shall pass ; for it shall be
Beyond the darkness horrible
    The Soul shall find new purity.

Like a lost child through ways untrod,
  Bitten of snake and torn of briar,
The Soul goes wailing after God,
  Whose light retreats and still shines higher.
Oh, where is God gone? Is He dead?
  Or shut in heavens beyond desire?

Out of the vileness lilies blow,
  Out of the graves new bodies rise;
Out of the anguish, who knows how?
  A nobler soul prays to the skies.
The Soul moves on with wounded feet
  Out of the adder-haunted wood;
Slowly the bitter heart grows sweet,
  And God's strength pulses through the blood.
God is not dead: He heals the soul,
  Seeing use in evil: He is good.

V.

THE SOUL'S RETURN.

LIKE a great ship the world moves on
  Through boundless seas of living blue;
Above, the glimmering of God's throne,
  Heaven's gates with angels looking through;

Around, the mighty fleet of stars,
  With spirits crowding deck and mast ;
And far beyond, the harbour-bars
  Of stillness where all meet at last.

And sickness wastes the crowded crew,
  And Death broods silent at the bridge,
While to the individual view
  The land grows like a shining ridge.
And sheer beneath the world's bright side
  The little boat of life is dropped,
And drifts upon the solemn tide :
  The world sails on, and has not stopped.

O mystery ! O miracle !
  The crowded ship is left behind.
That moment—ills we know too well ;
  And this—broad calm and gentle wind.
And ever the boat goes gliding on,
  And in it lies the frozen dead :
The father's child, the widow's son,
  Who now is God's alone instead.

The frozen body lies all white,
  With votive flowers wreathed round the head ;
With closed sunk eyes, whereon the light
  Breaks, but wherefrom the light is fled.

And shining at the boat's prow stands
  The human Soul, an angel bright,
A child-form, lifting eager hands
  Towards distant shores beyond the night.

The glimmering coast-line rises up ;
  God's chamber-windows, open wide,
Fill the deep voids, as wine a cup,
  With golden light.   And on the tide
The boat that bears the dead lies like
  A floating spot of dark ; alone
Upon the Spirit's face there strike
  The shafts of morn.   The boat moves on.

" O world, farewell !" the lifted lips
  Sighed forth ; and then at some dumb sign
The body leapt up from eclipse,
  And stood triumphant and divine.
" O world, farewell !   Thy passionate pain
  Hath worked its holy miracle ;
God toileth long, but not in vain,
  And lo ! He doeth all things well."

" *Farewell !*"   Through deep wells of that sea
  The word sunk dying ; but within
This darkened world I saw the free
  Glad light of morn through mists of sin.

I saw the vision of what should be,
   The face of God that all-sufficed ;
And heard, clear through earth's mystery,
   A multitude who sang of Christ.

VANDERDECKEN.

" THE hornèd moon hung low last night,
On the world's edge it poured its light.

" Between its tips the shadow lay
Of the old moon now burned away.

" Around it ran a rainbow-rim
Of many colours, but all dim.

" Like a black shore the tempest lay
Along the water's ashen grey.

" It changed, and seemed a vast sea-snake
Hungering in a good ship's wake.

" It spread its jaws, like gates of hell
To catch the wan moon when she fell.

" It changed, and like a hand became,
With many fingers spurting flame.

2

"It quenched the waning moon, and shot
Its light where now the moon's was not.

"A moan ran through the glassy sea,
And than the wind fell suddenly.

"Good master! this did hap last night,
It was a vision of affright.

"May Christ have mercy, master dear,
For the hour of storm and death is near!"

The skipper laughed, and blithely said:
"No wind that ever blew I dread.

"Ho! mate, your thoughts run all amiss:
When was a goodlier night than this?

"Last night the wind fell; but to-night
The sail swells, and the breeze is light.

"Last night the horned moon on the sea,
Lay deep in shadow and mist, may be.

"To-night I saw her rise and float
Along the sea's edge, like a boat.

"Above her silver prow burned bright
One star, hung like a drop of light.

"Her long rays shot like silent oars
Across the ocean's gleaming floors.

" Ho! mate, the night is fine and clear ;
Never had man less cause for fear.

" Thrice have I sailed around the Cape ;
I fear not storm, nor demon's shape !"

" Good master, hark ! I saw but now
A bird fly past, as white as snow.

" I saw a light burn on the mast ;
It quivered, and went out, as she passed.

" I saw a light spread in the sea,
And looked, and lo ! fair vessels three.

" At the sea's bottom dead men lay,
Waiting the break of the Judgment Day.

"Their cheeks were sunk, their brows were white,
Their eyes were open in the light.

" O master dear, the light breeze fails !
These are the seas the Dutchman sails.

" No wind that ever blew, I fear :
But the Phantom Ship, 'tis sailing near !"

Loud laughed the scornful skipper, and said :
" Let fools believe in a Ship of the Dead.

" If such there be, God answer me,
I meet her to-night upon the sea.

"For if such be, and luck befall,
I'll sail right through her, decks and all.

"And the ship of living fools I sail
Shall grapple her dead fools, old and pale."

The ship stood still, as though it was
Frozen within a sea of glass.

Like a dead thing the ship has stopped:
Into the sea the moon has dropped.

Over the sea a black mist rolled,
Muffling the ship's bell as it tolled.

So dark it was, we could not see
Each other's forms at paces three.

Then suddenly a little waft
Of hot air struck the ship abaft.

The sea broke into flame, and now
The wind drove through it like a plough.

A cloud of fiery spume flew first,
Then came the long deep wave, and burst.

Above its falling crest and side
A snow-white bird flew low, and cried.

Like stubble swept from a threshing-floor
The good ship fled that gale before.

Hoarse cried the skipper, "Ho! comrades ten,
Hold fast, and face the gale like men."

None made him answer, for each one
Stood still, as he were turned to stone.

Hoarse cried the skipper, "Right ahead
I see a ship's light burning red!"

None made him answer; each man knew
The Phantom Ship was close in view.

Before our very bows she ran:
No voice rose from us, boy or man.

Her rotten sails hung loose o'erhead,
Her deck was crowded with the dead.

Straight stood each man with waxen face,
Straight stood each man within his place.

Dumb was that ghostly company;
But Vanderdecken laughed for glee.

His eyes burned like a fire, and proud
Upon the poop he stood and bowed.

"Ahoy!" he cried; "what year is this?
Since first I sailed, Time's clock's amiss.

"Vanderdecken of Amsterdam,
All the world knows who I am.

"All the world, so green and broad,
Do its good folks still believe in God?"

Louder the black wind roared and blew;
We cut the Phantom Ship in two.

Her deck of the dead broke into twain,
And rose above us, and met again.

Into her shadowy spars I leapt;
Under my feet the good ship swept.

I saw the skipper stand alone,
And all his men as turned to stone.

A well of light sprang in the sea:
At the sea's bottom were good ships three.

I looked again; on the sea's floor
Were many dead men, and good ships four.

I alone was the saved. Ah, me!
Better to rot in the slime of the sea.

A living man, with a crew of the dead,
I sail on the ship of doom and dread.

The wind of God's anger smites the sea,
But shriller rings Vanderdecken's glee.

Every time that a ship goes down
The dead men move, and their faces frown.

Every time a ship gets home
Vanderdecken curses his doom.

And the dead men with their lips all grey,
Touch my lips that I cannot pray.

So I sail, and I cry in vain
For the Judgment Day to end my pain.

THE BALLAD OF THE DEAD MOTHER.

WHY is it the baby will not sleep,
Albeit the time has come for sleep?
   All day its little lips have cried,
   All day the wind has risen and sighed
And snow has fallen, and lies full deep,
   And now it is eventide.

The mother is dead : we buried her
A month ago, and wove her hair
   In a golden pillow, and folded her hands
   Like the hands of the Blessed Mother who stands
In the crimson church-window at prayer,
   And we laid her babe for a minute's space
   Across her frozen bosom and face,
But yet she did not stir.

But when we lifted the babe again
  The mother's purple eyelids stirred,
  And it seemed she knew, it seemed she heard,
(For the babe was crying again),
  It seemed she knew, and her dead ears heard,
And her heart beat once for pain.

The risen moon was shining now
  Over the wild white waste of snow ;
  Through the bare windows burst the glow,
  And the flakes of light, like flakes of snow,
    Drifted about her hollowed face,
And lay upon her brow.

Why is it the baby will not sleep,
Albeit the hour for sleep has come ?
  We heard the wind cry over the plain,
  On the dead mother we looked again :
Half of her face now lay in gloom,
For the moon had moved across the room ;
And every time the baby cried,
She seemed to turn her head aside,
  And her mouth moved as in pain.

A month it was from the burying-day,
The great snow-clouds in heaven were gray,
 And the moon came wearily wading through ;
  At last the little one fell asleep,
 The foster-mother was sleeping too,
  And the weary moon was wading deep,
A month from the burying-day.

A month and a week, and every day
The babe was crying its life away ;
But now each night, just as the moon,
Like a naked spirit with silver shoon,
 Came gliding between the files of fir ;
The little one waked no more with woe,
 But lay as still as the heart of her
Who was fast asleep in the kirkyard snow.

I woke and watched, and first I saw
A bank of leaden cloud withdraw,
 And the moon's rim glimmered and sank :
And then a little surf of light
Ran over the floor of hyaline,
 And the stars hushed rank on rank ;
And then two high bare crags between
 The light came like a tide.

Fast asleep was the foster-mother,
I was awake, I, and no other ;
  All the world slept beside.

And then I heard a voice that spake,
I being the only one awake,
  And heaven not far away ;
And I saw the lonely mother stand
Like Mary upon Christ's right hand,
  And I heard the angels pray.

Far off upon those coasts of heaven
O dost thou steal away at even,
  To hide from God and weep ?
And is it because thy heart doth know
  Thy little birdling cannot sleep
In the lonely world below ?

Yea ; well I know this must be so,
  Thou sing'st no litanies :
Yea ; God the Blessed Son doth know
  How even in heaven a baby's cries
  Make mothers' eyes o'erbrim ;
For God the Blessed Son doth know
  How His mother lovèd Him.

And He who made the moon and stars,
   Being once as thy little one,
Will He not say, " O mother sweet,
The moon-waves shall bear up thy feet,
   In the name of Christ the Son ;
Go to thy babe a little while,
And teach his lips to sleep and smile,
   Do all thou would'st have done :
And all this will I grant to thee,
For the sake of the Mother who lovèd Me,
   When I was a little one"?

Through all the stars 'tis but one step
To the mother who hears her infant weep,
   And the babe shall sleep at last ;
A bar of moonbeams lifted was,
That the mother with folded hands might pass,
   And outward she hath passed.

Through all the stars, through all the waste
Void fields of air, the mother in haste
   Flies onward to her mark ;
And her heart is glad when that which was
A star of fire in a sea of glass
   Grows near, and vast, and dark.

'Twas just between the files of fir,
I saw at the window the dead mother,
    With the moon behind her head ;
Her lips and eyes were stilled with prayer,
And the moonlight drifted in her hair
    As it did when she lay dead.

Upon her brows a little ring
Of lovely light lay shimmering,
    Her face was full of rest ;
And when she stepped out of the night
The babe smiled upward to her light,
The babe looked up, then closed his eyes,
For he drank the dews of Paradise,
    From her full heart and breast.

The little one hath fallen asleep,
    The day breaks gray and slow.
    All day the babe wakes, and doth know
    His mother is coming over the snow,
    And chasms of death, that lie between
    The kirkyard clay and heaven's green,
And the snow of death is deep.
    All day the babe shall cry for woe,
But at night the babe shall sleep.

There, at the feet of God's own Son,
   She singeth now meek litanies;
   And waits until the Master's eyes
   Droop on her, and He saith, " Arise,
For on earth the day is done !"

There, at the feet of Christ, she prays,
Waiting until the Master says,
   " I have heard thy little one :
Thy babe it wakes all day and cries,
   For love of its mother dear ;
For love of its mother dear it cries,
   And its cry is sad to hear.
Go forth in the name of the Blessed Son,
   And on earth a little while,
   Teach thy babe to sleep and smile ;
And all this will I grant to thee,
For the sake of the Mother who lovèd Me,
   When I was a little one."

The angels crowding in God's light,
   Behind heaven's lifted bars,
Are watching the mother in her flight
   Along the road of stars.

But the Mother of Christ is not with them,
She sitteth still within her place,
And I know by the look upon her face
She is thinking of Bethlehem.

THE DELUGE.

I.

DARK as a mist on dying eyes
    The night crept through each street and square
Death-dumb and drear against the skies
    The city towers stood cold and bare.
The swooning air lay thick and still
    Upon the groves of clove and musk,
And dying winds blew down each hill
    Dead vapours through the stifling dusk.

II.

List now, my sons, strong sons of mine,
    Who rule and fill an empty earth—
List, ere this fluttering breath divine
    Return to Him who gave it birth.
For I have walked a weary way,
    And now, like one who wholly spent
Sees palm-trees gleam above the spray
    Of fountains, I would die content.

The Deluge.

III.

Dark as a mist on dying eyes
   I saw the gloomy night roll down ;
Far off, unto my ears the cries
   Of drunken mirth and hate were blown.
Fierce horror tore the silent dark
   Of murdering knave, and murdered dolt,
While I within my lonely ark
   Stood waiting God's first thunderbolt.

IV.

Like one who stands and sees at dawn
   The smoke of burning cities cloud
The saffron skies, so, far withdrawn,
   I saw the great world in its shroud.
All white as smoke the hot mist crept
   O'er mountain steeps, and street, and home ;
And on each peak there burned and leapt
   The pallid lightning-fire of doom.

V.

Loud rose the riot and died away
   In laughter such as chilled the ear,
The face of Lust grew gaunt and gray
   With agonies of mystic fear.

For all the heavy air was thick
　　With quivering sound, and no star shone ;
The very earth moaned and was sick,
　　And still the mist came rolling on.

VI.

Ah, waking mother ! closer grasp
　　Thy child ; O babe, drink to the lees
The bosom's life, ere God unclasp
　　The belt that holds the land and seas.
Ah me ! and while they strain and hark,
　　And pierce the dark with eyes of fire,
I hear around my lonely ark
　　The wailing water-floods creep nigher.

VII.

The river lapped along the shore,
　　The far sea moaned as if in pain ;
A broad low rim as red as gore,
　　The moon lay dying on the plain.
I knew not if I waked or dreamed,
　　My breath with stifling fear was stopt ;
No thunder broke, and thick there steamed
　　A blood-like dew, and on me dropt.

VIII.

O God! to see a single star
　Through purple glooms swim up the sky;
Of all the fearful things that are,
　'Tis worst in dark and dread to die!
Of all the fearful things that crush
　The brain, 'tis worst to stand and wait
In helplessness the cataract-rush
　Of the avenging deeps of fate!

IX.

The spotted leopard in his lair
　Moaned like a child; the snake upreared
Her dappled crest: an awful glare
　Was in her eyes; each creature feared.
The birds were dumb, the cattle lowed,
　And far within the deepest dark
The lion's dreadful eyeballs glowed
　As they would burn the very ark.

X.

The fluttering dove could find no peace;
　A sad wind moaning round her nest
Stirred her unquiet wings; no ease
　Was there, nor calm, nor any rest.

The raven croaked, the eagle flapped
  His wings on air confined and dun,
Remembering mountains thunder-capped,
  And restless to behold the sun.

XI.

Then shattering thro' the dark there broke
  A sound, far off, that nearer rolled :
A surge of wind, a cry that woke
  All flesh, a noise of bells that tolled
Above the clouds.   And lo ! a hand
  With fire and glory veined and starred
Thrust to my door ; with bolt and band
  Of ringing crystal it was barred.

XII.

The beasts lay death-still in the light,
  With flaming eyes that smouldered red,
Like watchfires on a lonesome night,
  All fixed on me in quivering dread.
And thro' the roar of rending skies
  The great Doom burst and drowned the moon
And groaning like a man who dies
  The earth lay—and the storm rolled on.

XIII.

Then sudden all my heart grew cold
  To hear an onward rush of feet.
Was it the wolf without the fold ?
  Or were they human hands that beat
Against the doors ?   And were they men
  Who prayed in vain ?   And did they cry
For help in their great fear, and then
  Pray only God would let them die ?

XIV.

I heard a miser drag his bags
  Of gold ; I heard a mother weep,
A beggar raving in his rags,
  A babe that moaned and died in sleep.
A mighty pity choked my throat.
  The beating hands waxed weak ; there swirled
A black strong wave ; I was afloat,
  And plunging o'er a drowning world !

XV.

My heart stood still, an icy sweat
  Broke from my flesh, the gathering fear
Closed on me like a tide, and yet
  No cry my lips could make !   And near,

Like cursed fiends, the wild beasts lashed
  And foamed, but voiceless they as I ;
The falling heavens in thunder crashed,
  And drowned the great world's dying cry.

XVI.

Then something snapped within the heart,
  Then something burst within the brain,
And I was mad.   I tore apart
  A door, and felt the rush of rain.
The heavens with running fires burned white,
  As though a thousand days were heaped
In awful light : and black as night
  O'er rocks of fire the cataract leaped.

XVII.

Black, black as night, save when the glare
  Pierced like a jaggèd sword straight through
The mighty flood, through burning air
  The hissing stream fell down, and threw
Far up a wreath of lightning-spray.
  O, vision terrible and grand !
And up the steep heavens, far away,
  In utter calm, I saw God stand.

XVIII.

And high above the whirlwind roar
  Of ruin pierced His awful voice,
" *Lo, I am with thee !*" Nevermore
  I heard it, but my instant choice
Clasped Him as with a dying hand ;
  And far away in prophecy
I saw the heights of Ararat stand,
  And God's great rainbow span the sky.

XIX.

Then dew-like calm possessed my brain,
  And lulled me like a little child
Who sleeps, and wakens from his pain
  Through simple weakness hushed and mild,
For like a cradle rocked the ark,
  While out of heaven a great wind blew,
And all at once I heard the lark
  Begin to sing, and on we flew.

XX.

And all the birds took up his note,
  And sang as in their native wood,
So strangely sweet with warbling throat,
  I wept to hear their happy mood.

I wept, and wondered if they knew
 The voice that spake, and inly stirred,
Sang worshipping : and was it true
 That I was deafer than the bird ?

XXI.

Then through my heart a gush of prayer
 Thrilled gently, and I knew at length
The great world like a babe most fair
 Was borne within God's arms of strength.
And shall I judge this thing He did,
 In Whom is righteousness alone ?
His pathway in the seas is hid,
 But lo ! His footsteps are not known.

THE BALLAD OF CAREW.

IT is the bridal chamber,
  To-night's the wedding-night,
And Lord Carew sits in his hall
  With his bonny bride so bright.

The wind is roaring round the tower,
  The gale comes on apace,
Lady Carew sits with her lord,
  But death-white is her face.

"And wherefore should thy cheek be pale,
  And wherefore tremble so?
Castle Carew is safe as heaven,
  Whatever winds may blow."

Paler grew the bride's pale cheek,
  The blue veins on her brow
Showed like buds of violets
  Buried amid the snow.

" It is not wind or rain I fear,
  It is not Castle Carew ;
I fear the evil blast that blows
  With woe for me and you !"
The web of doom is spinning.

It is the bridal chamber,
  The maid Janet is there ;
She is but serving-maid, yet sooth
  The maid Janet is fair.

She stands and hears the singers sing,
  She hears the dancers tread,
She stands all in the dark and hears
  With heart that's like to lead.

"Cursed be the bonny bride," she cries,
  "And cursed be Lord Carew,
Because of this sore wrong to me,
  Ye have agreed to do.

" How can ye with the feasters sit,
  And know what ye do know ?
My shame is thine, O Lord Carew !
  And thine shall be my woe.

" Thy bonny bride shall dance to-night
    To music fast and blithe ;
She is thy bride, O Lord Carew !
    She shall not be thy wife.

" Ye two shall sit within the hall,
    And drink the wine so red,
But only one shall lie to-night
    Within the marriage-bed !"

The maid Janet stands all alone
    Within the bride-chamber ;
The dancers all are dancing now,
    And no one misses her.
The web of doom is spinning.

It is the bridal chamber,
    The bride hath said her prayer,
It is the maid Janet who takes
    The bride-jewels from her hair.

" And did ye think on Lord Carew
    When ye did bow an' pray ?"
" Indeed I thought on none beside
    Upon my wedding-day !"

" And did ye pray to sleep full well,
    And did ye pray aright ?"
" Full little thought of sleep had I—
    It is my wedding-night !"

Maid Janet flings the jewels down,
    She rises to full height :
" O deep will be thy sleep, an' long,
    On this thy wedding-night !

" The marriage-bed is broad and white,
    The bed is fair to see,
The linen sheets I spread for two,
    They are no' broad for three.

" The marriage-bed of Lord Carew
    Was made two years ago,
And Lord Carew hath wrought my shame,
    And his shall be my woe !"
The web of doom is spinning.

It is the bridal chamber,
    Within the marriage-bed
The bride is sleeping deep and long—
    Lady Carew is dead.

The Lord Carew knocks at the door,
    His voice is blithe with pride ;
" And may I now come in ?" cries he,
    " And may I see my bride ?"

It is the maid Janet who says,
    " Come in, my Lord Carew ;
I have undressed your bride, my lord,
    And she is fain for you.

" Step in, and say was ever bride
    On wedding-night so gay ?
She's fast asleep, and will wake up
    In the dawn o' the Judgment Day !"
The web of doom is finished.

STRADIVARIUS.

O WORKER, I see thee; all eager thy face with its
passion,
Lined grimly, God-lighted, bent over the work thou
dost fashion.

Like His is thy look, who lighted the stars and
made splendid
The void with His glory, and smiled that His
labour was ended.

For His smile, like a sunshaft, has run through the
dark world forever,
And lit the stern brow of each worker who rests
from endeavour.

But why so pale and so angry, my toiler, my master?
What! is it a rift or a crack that betokens disaster?

Well, varnish will heal it : what odds, if it find but
    a buyer ?
"*Not so,*" cries my worker, and lo ! his words burn
    like a fire.

" Let those lie in veneer who toil basely for wage of
    the Devil,
But better to work not at all, than make the work
    evil."

So he shatters his work, and toils on with Pro-
    methean vigour,
And the light on his face is the light that doth
    cleanse and transfigure.

Ear-downward I see him, intent, while the lithe
    anxious finger
Sweeps over the strings, in whose dumbness such
    harmonies linger.

Then mellow as song of the thrush in the stillness
    of even,
Or clear as the voice of a child singing far up in
    heaven ;

Or sad as the wail of a world heart-broken and
dying,
The magical sounds burst, yearning and soaring
and sighing.

And gladder the light on his face, as the chords
throb, till slowly
It spreads like a sunrise, and broadens and glows
clear and holy

Amid the confusion and dust, till the workshop
seems rather
A niche of God's heaven, made bright by the
Infinite Father,

Whose angels, like flakes in a snowstorm of glory,
unnumbered,
Crowd silent, to hear this new song that for ages
had slumbered.

O worker of workers, toil on ! thy reward shall be
given
In knowledge of labour well done, which for brave
men is heaven.

Yea, after thy fingers are dust, thy spirit translated
Shall hear the world ring with the music thy
  patience created.

Wherever the heart of the poet, the thought of the
  master
Find speech through thy work, thy heart shall beat
  gladder and faster ;

Till angels, beholding thy face, shall know by the
  spasm
Of quick-pulsing glory that lights it, how up the
  vast chasm

Of star-crowded void thou hast heard the thrilling
  and wailing
Of chords thou did'st fashion long since with labour
  unfailing.

A STREET VISION.

THE glare of the gas just caught her face,
  Striking it full and even ;
To me it smote like a shaft of light,
  From the eyes of God in heaven.

The tawdry flower, and the weary smile,
  And the eyes with their rings of pallor,
Bespoke in a tongue whose words are fire
  The bankrupt heart's wild squalor.

Pass her not with a shrug of scorn,
  The human is still the human ;
Think how Christ had a mother once,
  And think how this waif is woman.

Who are you, to push her aside,
  You, with a heart untempted ?
Virtue is scarcely virtue that stands
  Because from trial exempted.

If Christ were walking this Strand, I think
   He would pause, and in all the city
Would find no soul towards whom He yearned
   With tenderer love and pity.

You hate her sin ?   And so does she,
   For what does sinning win her,
But daily hell ?   And hating sin,
   Yet God hates not the sinner.

I saw when the gaslight struck her face
   A meaning you did not gather ;
My heart stood still : for years ago
   My friend of friends was her father !

IN A SICK-ROOM.

SAINT AND UNBELIEVER.

UNBELIEVER.

I AM weary of conflict with doubt, I am faint with
    the woe of desire,
The threads of my brain are worn thin, and they
    melt like wax in a fire;
I am weary of trying to think that what I am think-
    ing is wrong,
For faith's sake trying to stifle a truth which is all
    too strong,
For faith's sake striving to think the thing that is
    not true is,
That I may buy with a lie a morsel of dying bliss.
Must I die with a lie on my lips, and is this the
    only way
Out of the fever and pain into the peace and the
    day?

SAINT.

O darling, I pray for your soul : will you not also
   pray?
However faint is the cry of the lamb that is lost in
   the snow,
The Shepherd of Souls will hear, and He was a
   Man of Woe !

UNBELIEVER.

A Man of Sorrows indeed, for was not His cry on
   the cross
A wail through the darkness of death, a moan of
   infinite loss ?
If He from the broken depths of that tender and
   pitiful heart
Wailed of faith that had failed, and hope that was
   swift to depart ;
Ah ! shall I weep and complain that I, who have
   lived in vain,
Lie dying as Jesus did, in isolation and pain ?

SAINT.

Hush, darling ! knowest thou not that He trod the
   wine-press alone,
That all the anguish of man by Him should be
   borne and known ?

Known in its infinite depths, its uttermost shame
    and dismay,
Borne with its infinite load, yea, utterly borne
    away ?

UNBELIEVER.

Ah, beautiful old belief ! How sweet to think it
    were so ;
I have heard my father pray when wasted and
    weak with woe,
And ever as he lay dying the same words made his
    prayer,
" Thou hast borne it away "—yet why has He
    borne it, and where ?

SAINT.

It is not for us to question ; enough for us that
    we trust——

UNBELIEVER.

Yet, wife, you know we think, not what we would,
    but we must.
It is vain to say to the mind, " Thus far and no
    farther go ;"
Vain as the vain king's boast to the sea with its
    ebb and flow.

The tide will rise by a law stronger than thrones
    and kings,
And a scornful laughter lives in its mighty
    thunderings,
And the white-lipped waves are crying, "'Twere
    well that kings were flying,
For we are the power of Law, with a mission to
    judge and slay
Even crowned king-fools if they venture to stand
    in our way!"
I can stifle no better my mind's sharp query-
    thrust
Than thou thy gentle heart, with its true and
    womanly trust.

SAINT.

O that thou wouldst believe!   So simple and easy
    it is,
And it brings such wonderful peace, and is such
    marvellous bliss.
Yet I know how true are thy words : deep and
    strong is thy brain,
And I cannot follow thy thoughts, and this has
    been ever my pain.

Even in those young days when first we were man
    and wife,
I felt there were secret rooms deep-hidden within
    thy life :
I dwelt in thy heart of hearts, but never was able
    to find
The clue that could lead me through the labyrinth
    of thy mind ;
And ah ! how many times I have wept in the night
    with fear,
And have kissed thy lips and prayed, when thou
    wert sleeping, dear,
And have wondered if indeed it were true that
    thou and I,
Who have lived together so long, should part when
    one should die,
Should part for ever and ever, because thou
    couldst not pray
And utter one word of faith, which is so easy to
    say !

UNBELIEVER.

Dear heart, we shall not part; if another life there is,
We shall never, never part—let us seal it with a kiss!

Let the creeds and preachers go, let the theologians
    sink,
God is better than we know, and is kinder than we
    think.

SAINT.

Dost thou indeed believe? For a light shines in
    thine eyes,
And thy words are like a saint's, simple, and strong,
    and wise!

UNBELIEVER.

O, I have sometimes thought,
    And I almost think it now,
Not merely is God kinder,
    But nearer than we know.
Then again the darkness closes,
    And the sunbeams waste and fall,
Like broken threads of fire,
    And the cloud is over all.
And deeper falls the gloom,
    Till from its depths the cry
Of immense and hopeless wailing
    Thrills the world with agony.

And I hear the stifled thunder
    Of a great machine called Law,
Grinding down the lives of men
    As machines grind worthless straw.
And I cry, Ah! what am I,
    That I should ever climb
Out of this whirlpool deep
    Up the slippery steps of Time?—
That ever I should speak
    Of a victory over death—
I, whose cry is like a gnat's cry,
    Whose life is but a breath!
That ever I should dream
    Of a God with tender lips
Kissing prodigals, and lifting
    Dying men from Death's eclipse!
It is vanity—no more,
    It is huge and blind conceit
Builds up this dream of living
    When the grass grows at our feet.
When the grass grows at our feet,
    And all the woods are green,
And our footsteps are effaced,
    As though they had not been,

When our bones are dust, and mix
    With the growth of grass and flowers,
And life within the daisy
    Is the only life that's ours,
And the birds sing in the heavens,
    And the waves break on the shore,
And the place and hearts that knew us
    Know us never, nevermore !

SAINT.

O that thou wouldst believe! So simple and easy
    it is,
And it brings such wonderful peace, and is such
    marvellous bliss!
Yet, I cannot think thou art lost, and wrecked like
    a ship in the night,
The harbour is reached in the dark as surely as in
    the light.
So good hast thou been to me, so patient and tender
    and true,
That I think whether saved or lost, I shall be safe
    with you !
Whether saved or lost, I know that never did
    nobler heart
Beat in the life of a saint, and a saint to me thou art :

And, God forgive me the thought, but O, my darling, I know
Your fate must ever be mine, and where you go I go!
How could I sing my hymns before the glory of God,
When all that was left of you lay rotting under the sod ?
How could I sit at peace in that rapture consum-mate,
When you with wasted lips were wailing at heaven's gate ?
And you are better than I : you, with all your doubt,
From the chords of life have smitten a nobler music out.
I have been full of fault, in spite of praying and creed,
And you without creed at all have been true in word and deed.
And so (forgive me, God !) but I seem to find new light,
For I see it is better to do than to believe the right.
And thou hast done the right, not knowing God's decrees ;
And now, whate'er befall, though the saints forsake us all,
Cast out with thee I'm safer than saved and crowned with these !

UNBELIEVER.

Nay : do not fear, sweet wife,
    God will never harm thee, dear,
Love is better than all creeds,
    And is stronger than all fear.
If for love's sake thou wouldst pass
    To the darkness and the flame,
Till for love's sake even these
    As the heaven of heavens became,
Do you think the Love of Loves,
    If He love no more than this,
Will not bless us with one smile,
    And greet us with one kiss ?
Lo ! many things grow clear,
    And I, too, have new light,
I think I shall not miss
    God's harbour in the night.
For I seem to see even now,
    Far across the livid foam,
A long light fall and spread,
    And it is the light of home.
It is wonderful to think
    That after all the Lord
May have pitied me and judged
    By my wish and not my word !

It is wonderful to think
  That while my lips denied,
He was breathing on me peace,
  And was standing by my side.
Light of Light and Love of Love,
  Higher, stronger than all Force,
He, the soul of all things,
  Holding all things in their course.
Hearing every oath
  On the darkened lips of men,
Loving not less surely
  Those who love Him not again!
Very wonderful it is,
  And I think it must be true,
Though after long denial
  It seems very strange and new
To awake and find the mind clear!
  I remember how I woke
From the fever's fierce delirium,
  Looked up once, and never spoke.
Too weak to lift a hand,
  Or cry, or turn my head,
Seemed to dream I was alive,
  And yet felt I might be dead.

And lay quiet in my weakness,
   With closed eyes a little while,
Till I felt like sunlight falling
   The nearness of your smile.
Then my leaden eyelids stirred,
   And for a moment's space
I saw your breathless lips,
   And your eager stooping face.
So I knew I was alive,
   And for very joy I wept,
Then, like a weary child,
   With my hand in thine I slept.
Draw yet a little nearer,
   And smile upon me now :
With thy hand in mine I sink
   In the death-sleep deep and low.
And another hand I feel,
   And I see another Face,
Bending through the blackness,
   Full of light and full of grace ;
And life's long delirium ends
   With its dreams and fancies wild,
And I fall asleep at last
   Like a weary little child !

SAINT.

Lower and lower I bend, deeper and deeper he
    sinks,

O that my soul could drink of the bitter water he
    drinks !

Deeper and deeper he sinks, but ever a light on
    his brow,

A smile on his wasted mouth as the bitter waves
    o'erflow !

Lower and lower I bend, till a waft of the air of
    death,

Blown from the water black, is mingled with my
    breath ;

And the strength of my hands ebbs out, and my
    dead floats forth between,

Forth on the waters of God to the pastures of
    living green !

Heart that criest, be still ! O think of the ease
    that is his !

He rests in God's wonderful peace, he tastes of His
    marvellous bliss !

THE TOWN OF ETERNAL MEMORY.

HIGH up there whirls the windy vane,
A golden sentry o'er the plain,
At watch through sunshine, storm, and rain ;
  The earliest light strikes o'er the hills
And smites the spire, while far below
  Dark mist the dripping valley fills,
And through the vale the brook runs slow.

Apart from men the quaint church stands,
As might a monk with praying hands
Uplift to bless earth's pilgrim bands ;
  And far below a crooked street
Basks in the lazy sun of June,
  While drowsily up through the heat
The hum of men floats, like a tune.

5

A jasmined thatch peeps here and there,
Whose sweet scent fills the languid air ;
A cot with windows quaint and square,
    A mouldering mansion past its prime,
With peeling pillars, old and brown ;
    So, stirless in the stream of time,
There stands and sleeps the little town.

Great cities have I seen ; far steeps
Of wilderness where Nature sleeps ;
Strange lights that hang o'er azure deeps
    Of half-enchanted seas, whose foam
Is fire, and whose green shores enclose
    The wealth of pearl and gold ; but home
The heart voyaged when each day arose.

Cleaving the wastes of alien skies,
Abreast the dawn, with clear sad eyes,
Homeward the dove of Fancy flies,
    O joy ! to see in flying gleams
That land of youth, and hear through tears
    Familiar sounds of birds, and streams
That rippled through departed years.

There never shone a silver star
So large as stars of childhood are,
When fair above a fleecy bar,
   Cloud-born, we first saw Venus leap ;
And while our eyes the wonder drank,
   There swam into the sea-like deep
Great constellations, rank on rank.

There never bloom in manhood's prime
The flowers we loved once on a time—
Ah, long ago!—the beds of thyme,
   And violets, and forget-me-not,
In Life's spring woods, where, oh! so long
   Ago, ere Life's great sun waxed hot,
We played, and piped our hopeful song.

Was it the skies were then more fair?
Or was it that the dewy air
Bathed fresh young brows unlined by care?
   O happy days! O happy youth!
When Life was all a miracle,
   And we had never learnt the truth
That blights the vision, breaks the spell.

When first Life's water turns to wine,
We know the miracle Divine,
Which later grows a barren sign.
   O sweet Capernaum of birth,
Where first on these new-lighted eyes
   There rose the vision of the earth,
Is this the charm that in you lies?

So let me muse.   I stand before
This ivied porch, this old oak door,
And tread this little room's white floor.
   I think I see my mother lie,
And I claspt to her ebbing breast;
   She pale and faint, about to die,
And I the little stranger-guest.

What fashion had the dying face?
And had she blue eyes meek with grace,
And golden hair that lit the place?
   And in her voice a mellow tone,
And on her brow a smile serene,
   This unknown mother, yet my own,
This mother, whom I scarce have seen?

Another foot is on the floor;
The good dame at the chamber-door
Cackles her gossip's simple store.
    Ah me !—the tears rush to my eyes;
I only hear a dying prayer;
    Cold lips pressed to a babe's who cries,
Such vision holds the white bed there!

*   *   *   *   *   *

Hark! how the bells ring out in tune,
A jocund glee, a rhythmic rune,
Waking the happy heart of June;
    And in the quivering interval,
In undertones, subdued and sweet,
    The brooks through all the valleys call,
And children's voices fill the street.

Through this small window, up the lea,
I see the church, the black yew-tree,
And Memory something more doth see:
    A bride, crowned with her orange blooms,
Shook with a storm of happy sighs,
    Who smiling walks between the tombs,
With God's light falling from her eyes.

The crowd fills all the village street ;
They fain would look upon their sweet,
And cast their flowers beneath her feet,
  That seek the untrod ways of life ;
Her white hand flutters to and fro
  Within his arm ;—he feels, dear wife,
Even now the flutter and the glow.

'Twas like a quivering bird at rest,
Whose little heart within its breast
Only desired Love's purple nest.
  Ah ! strange sweet trick of sense and brain,
I hear again the village choir,
  My heart aches with a happy pain,
My life burns with a subtler fire.

And I remember all the day :
The hush of heart, the dawning gray,
The joy that scarce left room to pray ;
  And, shining like a light at sea,
Through dark dead years, above them all
  The sweet young face that smiled for me.
Ah me ! the happy tears must fall.

Each mossy lane could tell its tale :
'Twas here we met ; I passion-pale,
And dared not speak, lest I should fail.
　　And there the first strange kiss ; and here
The flower I plucked to deck your hair ;
　　The brook sings with your voice, my dear,
And your footprint is everywhere.

And years have fled since then, and we
Have made our home beyond the sea,
And now—a little wearily
　　We walk the world ; but though we die
Far off, and not in English earth
　　Sleep hand in hand, yet you and I
Yearn daily towards our land of birth.

And in the drowsy tropic calm
We see down weary groves of palm
A dream that soothes us like a psalm :
　　Green hedge-rows shaken by the breeze,
The dappled sunlight on the lawn,
　　And dipping o'er the chestnut trees
A day-moon in the lap of Dawn.

The bells ring slower o'er the lea,
The sun drops down into the sea,
At last the labouring world is free.
    And now I seem to see thee stand,
Dear wife, with face of matron-calm,
    And round thy knees in our far land,
Sweet lips sing low the evening psalm.

The wedding light yet fills thine eyes ;
But through their depths, blue as the skies,
The bride's glance of abashed surprise
    Breaks not ; but larger than of old
They gleam with quiet blessedness,
    And well I know that now they hold
Love deeper than we once could guess.

Ah ! since those fair sweet days of old
Thy heart has opened, fold on fold,
Like a white rose-bud filled with gold ;
    For mother's tears have been its dew,
And children's smiles have been its light,
    While wondrously it grew and grew
In statelier passion day and night.

And now the mystery grows more clear,
And I behold how year by year
We close and closer grew, my dear,
   And that great love of long ago
Was but the rapturous pain of birth;
   And what we were we smile to know,
Love hath so grown in strength and girth.

I thought Life's consummation come,
When through the crowd's applauding hum
With stifled breath I led thee home;
   When truly Life's small firmament
Held but one trembling orb hung low,
   Hope, like a prophet of content,
That burned each day with warmer glow.

But all the stars pressed fast behind,
Blown on, like ships, by some great wind:
Too sudden light had made me blind;
   And therefore one by one they came,
And now I see, with chastened view,
   My broadened skies are all aflame,
And heaven itself is breaking through.

Draw near, dear wife.   The evening hymn
Has died away ; the church is dim ;
Far off there dips the moon's red rim.
   In this great sacramental hush
God lights the altar-fires of heaven,
    And far away Life's cataract-rush
Sounds fainter in the depths of even.

Draw near ; lean to me o'er the seas,
And breathe this wholesome English breeze,
And kneel with me on bended knees.
   Beneath this church's shadow, you
Know how we brought the little child
    Who breathed, and died, and never grew,
When winter winds blew hoarse and wild.

And I have found the sacred spot,
And planted sweet forget-me-not,
Like fair prayers round the little cot
   He slept in once ; for I foresee
How your first whisper, through your tears,
    Of him and of his grave will be,
This baby hope of vanished years.

Sweet little face, I see you yet
In that last sleep so white and set,
The lash with baby-tears still wet ;
    And touching your small grave so green,
A reverent Fancy fires my life,
    And guesses what you might have been
Had you but lived to share our strife.

O little town ! sleep on, sleep on ;
Thou too hast heard life's joy and moan
Surge like the waves on coast-lines lone ;
    Raptures and agonies are thine,
The marriage-feast, the funeral,
    Life's water, and its bitter wine
Pressed by the woes that come to all.

The world rolls faster than of yore :
Fierce are the fires that melt life's ore ;
The thunderous stream rolls *past* thy door,
    And men despise thy drowsy toil.
But I, for dear days gone before,
    Love every inch of thy fair soil,
And thou art sacred evermore.

LONDON.

I.

O CITY of curse and splendour,
   City of wealth and pride,
Greater than any Venice
   Ringed by the salt sea-tide;
Mate of the ancient Athens,
   Where grew the brain of the world,
What time with calm high pæans
   Truth's banner was first unfurled;
Lo! wisdom, and lo! corruption,
   Knowledge and vice are thine,
Streets paved with the gold of commerce,
   Running with misery's wine;
Grandeur of church and palace,
   Horror of alley and slum,
Luxury vaunting splendours,
   Agony sitting dumb;

Temples made sweet with singing,
  And by-streets loud with curse,
So near—one amen ringing
  Crowns blessing and oath—and worse!
O City of infinite contrast,
  Heart of the wide vast earth,
Bring thy misery nearer,
  Hush thy chorus of mirth,
And still for a little moment
  The roar of thy streets of stone,
While a modern poet sings thee
  A poem that is thine own.

II.

When the country lad comes limping
  Into thy crowded ways,
With tired eyes taking for glory
  The gas-light's brilliant blaze ;
O cruel and awful City,
  What wilt thou do with him ?
For when hadst thou any pity
  For blue eyes heavy and dim ?
For the footways all are crowded,
  And the streets are thick with wheels :
Who thinks of a lonely stranger
  In a City where nobody feels ?

Faces laughing with revel,
  Faces sharpened with care,
Faces weary and reckless,
  That once were sunny and fair :
All in the whirling tumult
  Flash upward, and then haste by,
And say, as they pass the stranger,
  "*'Twere better that thou shouldst die !*"
For the stony streets are bitter
  When the City is fast asleep,
And the river runs black and coldly—
  Death's river is not more deep.
We shudder to hear its plashing,
  And homeless here by night—
'Twould make thy mother in heaven
  Weep, could she see the sight ;
And if the hem of thy garment
  But catch in the great machine
That weaves the City-splendour,
  It draws thee in between,
Like food for the mouth of a dragon,
  And crushes thee, muscle and bone ;
And none in a mighty City
  Will mourn for the loss *of one.*

III.

The ships lie thick in the river,
　The warehouses teem with food,
The shops are crowded with dainties,
　But on the pavement is blood !
And over the City gleaming
　The golden cross stands high ;
Alas that it comes no nearer
　To those who suffer and die !
The chariots roll in grandeur
　Through square, and city, and park,
And what know they who fill them
　Of miseries done after dark ?
The theatre-doors are crowded,
　The music is heard within,
But under the lighted archway
　Cowers the shadow of sin.
There is sound of clapping and laughter,
　For the actor has hit their mood :
" Was ever the song sung better ?
　Was ever the jest so good ?"
And outside, freezing and cursing,
　Garnished with tawdry and paint,
Who are these hungrily waiting,
　These, from whose raiment a taint

Floats like an air of the charnel,
  Spreading impalpable death,
Slaying our sons and our daughters
  With bitter and poisonous breath ?
The work of thy hands, guilty City,
  Doves once with plumage like down,
Whom thou hast made ravens and vultures
  To feed on the flesh of the town !

IV.

Poor soul! the soiled work of thy Maker,
  Whom once He pronounced very good,
Let such as are sinless abhor thee,
  And stone thee—if any man could !
So eager to barter thy body,
  And dost thou find sinning so sweet?
Ah, no ! thou art starving and sinnest,
  And the way is sore to thy feet.
O what if thy mother should see thee
  Clothed in thy silken shame,
Drunk with the wine of folly,
  Branded with open blame!—
The sweet mouth coarsened with curses
  That drew the milk from her breast,
The brazen laugh of the harlot
  On lips she once caressed,

The blue eyes once uplifted
  In childish faith and prayer,
Corrupt with hideous meaning,
  Hollow with lust and care.
Ah, God ! I hear her saying
  (And her words are her heart-beats),
Better dead in the cradle,
  Than damned in the London streets !

V.

O City of curse and splendour,
  Thy singer is choked in his song ;
He sees no long procession
  Of wealth go sweeping along,
But the crowd of faded faces,
  And the weary eyes of the lost,
Turned up a moment in praying,
  Then whirled by, passion-tost !
O men ! by the little children
  Clinging about your knees,
O priests ! by your gifts of healing,
  Have ye no help for these ?
Come down and look on your City,
  Befouled by the lust of man,
And if ye would preach Christ's Gospel,
  Begin where He began !

SOOT AND DIAMONDS.

THE story soon is told.   I am not one
Given to the melting mood, in haste to try
The pathos of my last new tender tale
Upon the first chance-comer ; but if you
Can hear me out indifferent, you are not
The human-hearted man I take you for.

The woman sinned, fell lower, as do her kind,
At last bore on her brows the devil's hoof,
Plain as though stamped in fire, and walked with
    those
Who make a public glory of their shame.
I had the chance of seeing her drama played,
Act after act, and write the story thus.

No woman sins for sin's sake.   First of all
Beside sealed gardens of delight she walks,
And hears the cunning whisper of love's lute,
And breathes the passionate air, and drinks the dew
Of honey from the bell of poisoned flowers,

Until the will lies slain within the heart,
Like the drained pulse within a dead man's hand;
And the brain swoons, and drags down in its fall
All judgment, reason, memory, leaving then
The fierce flesh like a tigress slipt from leash,
Triumphant, and athirst, past all restraint.
Then comes the fiery carnival, the burst
Of new sensations, the mad stripping off
To the last rag of every decent care,
In mere excess of fierce abandonment;
The whirl of feet within the ring of hell,
When the fiend grasps his conquered human soul
From out the crowd, and threads his lightning way
Among the dancers, ever drawing close,
And closer yet, the chasm where all sink
At the first warning stroke of Judgment's bell.
Well, this frail soul for sure passed through such paths
Felt vibrating along all chords of sense
Such rapture as the devil hides in sin;
And woke at last, grovelling pale and dumb
Within that judgment-light which conscience strikes
Already through the steaming vales of lust.

But the real point on which conjecture dwells
Is this, no more. We mark out human souls

Into two hostile camps, between whose tents
The great gulf yawns—the one being wholly good,
The other wholly and for ever bad—
Whereas the camps so near together lie
That they merge into one. Or put it thus :
The shot silk of our life casts off its light,
Not from its golden threads alone ; for who
Can say wherefrom the exact refraction springs,
Or mark the spot where shadow always lies ?
All threads meet in the fabric's general whole ;
The crimson sometimes less than crimson glows,
The soiled gray's sometimes sifted with fine light,
Or, in a word, the good is less than good,
And the bad better than the thing it seems.

The woman sinned, fell lower, as do her kind ;
From circle unto circle of her hell
Sank like a stone ; at last stood forth unshamed,
The City's sorceress, whose spider-snare
Was laid for wealthy innocence, whose flesh
Was fattened on the hearts' blood of her slain.
She had a child, whose glad young angel-face
Caught all heaven's light, and left the mother dark
The child fell ill, and then—mark, this is true—
This Jezebel, this slayer of men's souls,
Closed her gilt doors, put out her flaring lights,

Flung her cards from her like a nest of asps,
Left all her diamonds for her maids to steal,
And sat alone within a darkened room ;
Went noiselessly, kissed the child's fevered lips,
Made the small golden head a resting-place
Upon her unclean breast, and nursed the boy
Like any honest mother of you all,
Until the child babbled a prayer, and died.
You would have said a mother's holy love
Could never thrive in such a heart as this.
Well, lilies strike their roots into decay,
And draw heaven's gold out of a prurient soil ;
Had not this woman heaven's deep mother-love ?
Then presently the sickness smote her down,
Ploughed thro' her splendid beauty seams of fire,
And lit the brain with phantasms of despair ;
Yet from her lips the accustomed talk came not :
She lay as calm as any holy saint,
And murmured tender language, such as soothes
A moaning child's pain ; aye, and even prayed,
As once she did in far-off Brittany
When rings the saintly Angelus ; and last,
Opened her dimmed blue eyes, and sighed a prayer
To see—what think you ?—why, her mother's face.
You would have said—well, many things no doubt,
Deductions of most wise philosophy,

The permanence of evil, the degree
In which the sense of right dies, being diseased.
I simply state the truth : this woman's robe
Of shame fell off her, as the clouds fall off
The white sides of the wading moon, and left
Her soul unsmirched by all the smoke of hell,
Bowing in tears above a wasting child,
And crying humbly for her mother's face!

Lastly the mother came, in humble garb,
With kindly wrinkled peasant face, and passed
All unsuspicious through the broad saloons
Whose walls ran with the leprosy of shame,
To the low bedside, kissed the blackened lips,
Wept o'er the blasted beauty, even to the last,
By virtue of her own meek spotlessness,
Unconscious of impurity : and then
Upon the mother's humble breast there droppèd
The daughter's splendid head, and so she died.

Diamonds are made of soot ; and I know not
How, when, or where, amid the charred remains
Of burnt out hearts, God's silent power steps in
And gives the crystallizing touch that makes
The diamond flash out from the thick black ash
But who dare say that this thing cannot be ?

SALOME.

NOT that I care so much, but who could tell
The issue, like a hungry lightning glare
Flasht from clear heavens? I never danced so well,
That said he, said they all. I feel my hair
Stir still with magic motions, perfumed wind
Lashed into eddies, beating on the bare
Smooth limbs and breast; and then I'throw behind,
Over my shoulder, so, a sudden glance,
And catch their faces smitten by its light
Into a hungrier circle. Then I smile,
And suddenly all the spirit of the dance
Consumes me, rends me, blots and blurs my sight
With a fiery wind, their great eyes all the while
Burning yet closer, eating into my heart.
Who cares what comes? There's nothing good nor
   vile.
The world whirls round, I'm lifted like a part

Of a giant whole ; a spirit's in my feet,
He rends my raiment, shakes my black hair down,
Smites my lips into song, so shrill and sweet
It frightens me.   Ah, that's my own, my own !
Limbs, hair, song, face, I know to-night to be
Most beautiful.   Look, my lords, there's a foot
Worthy a throne at least !   What's the decree ?
Half of his kingdom Herod gives to me ?
I cannot tell ; but all the great lamps shoot
An angry light, and suddenly, like a tide,
The fire runs out of my heart, and still I stand
As though I had never moved ; and there's a hand
Laid on me, and Herodias, crafty-eyed,
Is buzzing at my ear.

What's a man after all ?   Is flesh so dear
That I should tremble ?   Yes, we feed on men,
You and I, mother ; that's a woman's part—
Glare on them, kiss them, draw them near, and then
Leave their bones to the vulture.   That's the art
You've taught me, and I have not learned amiss :
I'll snare a Cæsar some day—there's a prey
Worthy the aim.   I ever took as bliss
The sight of death.   Heart of me ! many a day

How I have clapped my hands to see the play,
When the stripped gladiators hewed and hacked
And made the sand red.   Once a man I saw
Just at my feet, torn by the lion's paw,
His shoulder bare to the bone, beseeching me
In a hoarse voice that was so shrill and cracked
I laughed outright.   'Twas god-like sport to see
The great beast leap, his angry mane like fire
Flashing about his ears, the downward stroke
Of the great foot striking into the mire
The man like a mouse, with his back torn and broke;
And I—I called for more—more lions, more men :
That tawny beast who glares in yonder den,
Pit him against a score, the supplest score
Of slaves who ever trembled !   Ah, the long day,
Would it had lasted longer !   Evermore
The same big pulse sending delicious thrills
Through the swoll'n veins, when the eye caught the
        ray
Of the sharp sword, and heard the lion roar
Over his prey, like thunder in the hills.
And Herod, you remember, all the day
Sleepily watched, quick'ning a little bit
When the men died, till through the narrow slit
Of his heavy lids you saw there burned a flame
Eager as mine, whose passion went and came

Like a strong madness, till I longed to hurl
You, and your Herod, and all the people down
Into the sand, and watch the bloody whirl—
I, on the topmost turret's slippery stone,
Standing triumphant in the wind, alone,
Watching you fight and die.   There, do not frown
That's but a fancy.   What was it you said?
This man, this John the Baptist: well, I own
I care not if he be alive or dead;
Let him rot slowly, or be slain, or choke;
But why should *I* strike the stroke?

I saw him once: dark like a thunder-rack
He lowered in the outer court, his eyes, jet black,
Burned with a flame no other eyes e'er had;
His voice like a trumpet, angry, somewhat sad,
Calling, *Repent:* I wonder what he meant?
There he stood garbed in skins, his shoulders bent
Black hair like mine, but grizzled and unkempt,
Looking around with something like contempt
Or pity, with a fixed, clear, eager gaze,
As one who saw right through the sunlight's blaze
Into the place beyond, where there are hatched
The viper-lightnings: so he stood and watched.

He moved me for a moment, made me feel
A strange deep thrill, I never could think why.
But you—you hate him with a hate so real,
I would not wonder if that same deep eye
Spied something now: or if those same thin lips
Loosed on you their sharp hail. I've heard it said
If you say "*John*" to Herod, he bows his head,
And his puffed face grows dark, as though eclipse
Breathed in the presence of a hated name.
Well, let him die: I never liked to see
Men whose eyes smote you with that kind of flame:
But why insist he die so secretly?
Now I would bring him in, call Tertius,
Make them both fight—there, in that marble space;
Think of what jest the two would make for us!
Only I just confess that solemn face
Might spoil the banquet with its angry eyes;
So why not save him for the lions? 'Twere wise
To keep a man like that; be sure he'd fight
Beyond the best. 'Tis hardly worth the light
To kill him secretly; we shall not see
Whether he quail or frown. But let it be.
We want no thunder-clouds round Herod's board;
Let them go quickly, bring the head abhorred,
And since you dare not bear it—*why, let me !*

MYSTERY.

WHAT phantasms move within life's chamber dark,
    And mock us with their vagueness and their light !
Cowled spirits now, whose deep eyes like a spark
    Burn fiery in the gloom: now flashing bright,
As though the lightning in their raiment ran ;
    Now dark and formless, but with lifted finger
    Of ghastly admonition, dim they linger
In the vast chasms of the heart of man.

To-day, from morn to eve, such Presences
    Have moved like broken lights within my brain ;
Have risen and fallen like the passionate stress
    Of music yearning with an endless pain ;
Have linked themselves about me like a fate,
    And yet have told me nothing, whispering only
    As winds that fail upon a wide plain lonely,
And sob along the ground when night is late.

When I arose at morn, upon me fell
  The sense and shadow of phantasmal fear,
Yet whence or why, it faileth me to tell;
  My life had gone back many an ended year,
And I stood silent by an angry sea,
  Looking in wonder on a sunset olden,
  That was not wildly red, nor calmly golden,
But wholly charged with light and mystery.

A belt of green along the horizon's line
  Held down the livid waves that chafed foam-
      lipped.
Above that spread a pale gold floor whose shine
  Changed at its western edge to fire, and tipped
Far peaks of cloud with anger; and again,
  Beyond all height the heaven's vast heart was
      riven,
  And crimsoned all that weird and windless even
With hints of an unutterable pain.

And on the cliff's edge, motionless and pale,
  I saw a woman with a fair young boy:
I knew her once, and oft her hidden tale
  Of shame, or sorrow, or departed joy,

Had sought to read in her averted eyes.
  But we had only met, and never spoken,
  And howe'er guilty or howe'er heartbroken
Were curious questions of my own surmise.

What did she here ?   Why after many a year
  Had memory kindled her pathetic face,
And joined it to that sunset full of fear,
  As though she found in that her proper place ?
What subtle witch within my brain had wrought
  This dream of Fate, which linked so close together
  That great sea-sunset with its angry weather
And this most lonely woman sorrow-fraught ?

Was that wild sky inwoven with human strife ?
  Its broken colours like a music strange
Set to the passion of her wasted life,
  Interpreting aright its depth and range ?
Did such a wan light flood her dying room ?
  Did such a livid sea her secret cover ?
  Was this the clue I never could discover,
Dropped fathoms deep, but plucked at last from
    gloom ?

Through all the loud hours of the busy day,
  Through all the slow hours of the sleepless night,
That sunset never wasted into gray,
  But flushed yet more intolerably bright ;
That woman with her child stood motionless
    Upon the cliff's verge as a ghostly column,
    And I was haunted by the vision solemn,
Of her immense, immeasurable distress.

And when I pause in many a day unborn,
  If such shall be, before some problem deep,
Baffled and faint, at Thought's dim verge forlorn,
  Then shall I see again that weird sky steep
With ghastly light that woman's lifted brow,
    And she shall stand above Time's sea unspeaking,
    For ever silent, though her heart be breaking,
Symbol of all we dream, but cannot know.

A LONDON SINGER.

HER face was very pale and sweet,
   Clear-cut, and full of candour :
Her voice had that strange bird-like note
   Which makes the fancy wander
To visions of blue skies, and glades
   Where brooks all day are singing,
And thrushes hidden in green depths
   Set all the woodland ringing.

Strange thought of mine ! In that loud hall,
   Amid the gas-lights' glitter,
Thus dreaming of the thrushes' song—
   Could satire be more bitter ?
But yet I felt some memory sad
   Of thrushes well might move her :
I saw the turf beneath her feet,
   The greenwood arched above her.

Poor child! while yet that fresh young voice
   Poured forth the music's passion,
Where was thy soul ?   What world of love
   Or memory didst thou fashion ?
I heard that wailing in thy voice
   Thou didst not strive to smother :
And didst thou see while singing there
   Thy old home, and thy mother ?

Perchance I think amiss, and waste
   My fancy and my pity ;
Thy childish feet trod no green fields,
   But pavements of the city.
Yet even so, 'twas Nature's plans,
   Made at the world's beginning,
That thou should'st sing in solitude,
   For brooks sing in thy singing.

And, O poor child ! if thou art here
   As some sweet bird the snarer
Hath lured away by baits of pride,
   O think, is life then fairer
Within this city's evil ways
   Than in those days departed ?
The thrushes call thee back to Devon ;
   Go, ere thou'rt broken-hearted !

LONDON VIOLETS.

HIGH above the thunder
  Of the roaring streets to-day
Pierced a thin and childish treble,
  Making all my pulses play
With new thrills of joy and longing ;
  For the voice was shrill and sweet
As a lark's voice, and its music
  Seemed to fill the long gray street.
And a sudden joy of sunlight
  Wandered through the heavy air,
And a sudden fragrance told me
  Far away the world was fair,
And I knew the spring had quickened,
  And down all the wind-swept hills
Rolled a tide of light and odour
  Yellow waves of daffodils,

Blue long waves of violets, crested
   With crocus white as foam,
And they flowed upon the city,
   To the very walls had come ;
For their broken scent and colour
   Came in, wandering every way,
While that childish voice was crying
   " Violets are cheap to-day !"

II.

And while I stood and pondered,
   In a vision I was lost ;
And I felt the warm air streaming,
   And the larks upon it tossed,
And I heard the buds all bursting,
   And I saw the gleaming sea,
And up the steep world flying
   Came the swallows wearily.
And then, first, the daisy watching
   On the cliff's verge steep and sheer,
Gave the signal they were coming,
   And the lark called loud and clear ;

And then all the woods were wakened,
　And the oak stirred in his sleep,
And the heart's blood of the primrose
　Gave a swift and happy leap,
And the blue-bells and the cowslips
　Joined their slender hands together,
And deep in hollows of the woods
　Danced with the windy weather:
And the pulse of men beat faster,
　Even in cities mirk and gray,
For the swallows back were flying:
　Violets were cheap to-day.

III.

Then suddenly that vision
　Faded,—and I stooped to see
How pale the eager messenger
　Who brought such news to me.
Had she seen the violets growing?
　Did she yearn to see again
The cowslips and the primrose
　Yellowing all the level plain?

Or rather some dim alley,
　Where no flowers could ever grow,
Some low room where child or mother
　Lay and wasted with their woe ?—
Was this the haunting vision
　Those blue eyes saw, evermore,
While she, the Spring's strange herald,
　Stood amid the City's roar,
Bringing sunlight, and sweet odour
　From a region far away,
With that shrill pathetic lark-cry,
　" *Violets are cheap to-day !*"

A DREAM OF RECOMPENSE.

In the first sleep of night, what time the wind
    Still stirs around the noisy wheels of thought
That slowlier turn, then stop, and leave the mind
    Like a great house made still; there came unsought

A vision or a dream, as though a child
    Did wander through my heart, and set again
The great wheels moving, just for antic wild,
    And ignorant of what was peace or pain.

First came strange music, like a choric song
    Heard faintly floating down a darkened sea,
Which the frail soul, driven by great winds along,
    Hears but a moment, ceasing suddenly.

Then flute-like voices like fair doves at play
    Filled all the air, flooding the azure calm;
Then with the gradual breaking of the day
    The vision of an island topped with palm.

All still it lay, as 'twere but yesternight
   God made it, and no waking bird dared break
The deep hush He had left, and clear white light
   Through golden mists fall on it streak by streak.

No gleam was there of any sun that shone,
   Or light of moon, or sky, or any star ;
But radiance surely of some crystal throne
   Shot earthward when heaven's gate is set ajar.

And then methought far on the highest lawn
   There moved a gliding figure robed in white,
Calm, with clasped hands, singing unto the Dawn,
   And so passed slowly, singing, out of sight.

Even as one who hears the bird of night
   Fluting her woes within the windy groves,
Feels all his sullen anguish with delight
   Melt into peace, that inly hopes and loves ;

And straightway is a little child again,
   Who runs glad-hearted through the copse and
     fallow,
Singing the light in with his simple strain,
   His wingéd soul light-fancied as the swallow ;

So always such sweet song filled all the air,
  And fell in dying gusts, and rose and swept
Through the clear deeps of heaven, with notes so
    rare,
  That lastly for my very joy I wept.

But when I followed breathless, crying aloud
  To know the singer's name, lo! evermore
The song outran me, lost within a cloud,
  And sometimes in the surges of the shore.

For in this isle of mystery there was
  Nought that was plain; the thin haze of my dream
Dimming all shapes and thoughts that strove to pass
  Before the spirit that felt their transient gleam.

And over peak and vale there moved and hung
  A drowsy air, that lulled the eager sense;
And singers were as though they had not sung,
  And guilt lapsed back again to innocence.

At length upon my eyes methought there fell
  The shadow of a presence, like a light
That wavers through a wood; and all the dell
  Wherein I brooded grew exceeding bright.

Then slowly through the mists the glint of hair
  That fell like twisted gold over the snow
Of a white vestal robe, burned on the air,
  While all the sea-like haze swayed to and fro,

Then broke like curtains suddenly withdrawn
  From a new star's fair front; and meek and calm
I saw an upturned face, fixed on the Dawn,
  That purpled through the silent groves of palm.

And straightway like a lute, whose spiritual chords
  Between the rush of worlds yearn mystical
In the deep night, her lips made silver words
  That held me captive in a happy thrall.

"Look on me, for thou knewest such an one
  Long since in your far world that dwells in gloom,
Lit with but fainting shadows of that Sun
  Wherein they dwell who triumph o'er the tomb.

"Flowers pine for light; souls weary in the shade,
  Until God pluck them; whereon all their hue
Deepens beneath His smile no more to fade;
  Behold who once I was!" I looked and knew.

A moment through the light there fluttered pale
  The vision of a wildered face, whose eyes
Burned dark with anguish ; then a chilly gale
  Swept her away through wastes of sunny skies.

Leaving a voice that wailed, " O weariness !
  O pain of love that sears the heart like fire !
What worse than love the bleak years never bless,
  Desire without the sweet fruit of desire ?

" Ah me, unhappy !   Sweet beloved, why
  Tarriest the morning ?   Through the dripping
    copse
Come quickly, that with earliest light we die,
  Ere yet the bells ring, or the skylark drops !"

As sometimes music with a sad refrain,
  Sung unto deafening ears of dying men,
Stirs the worn chords of memory in the brain,
  So her wild-words ; and I remembered then

Her tale of pain.   That story all men know ;
  How vowed to unblest rites, the heart that will
Love as it wills and where, blind with its woe
  Of loving hopeless, chose the lesser ill

Of death with him she loved, rather than bliss
  Of a polluted life cursed with the gold
Of a gray dotard, whose unholy kiss
  Were as the seal of honour bought and sold.

Wherefore when matin bells filled all the air
  With hollow glee, meanwhile the fateful day
Coming up slow and still, so deadly fair
  It breathed disaster; suddenly rang a gay

Shrill voice upon the topmost stair, and cried
  That the bride was not there! Then the whole
    house
Arose in fear, pale-staring, wonder-eyed,
  Yet dreaming of their broken morning's drowse.

And with fierce hubbub broke into that room
  Never before invaded thus. And there
All things lay hushed in a sepulchal gloom
  Of blinded windows ; flowers to dress her hair

Dead on the floor; while her white wedding-dress
  Hung ghost-like fluttering in the sombre air ;
'Twas like a death-room in its loneliness,
  Only they could not find the sweet dead there.

Then rushed they forth across the dewy park
  Crying aloud; some weeping, most indeed
Curious to find a scandal; till in the dark
  Wood's mossiest nook all stopped. You heard
    a seed

Come tinkling down, you heard the pine-bark
  crack,
  So deep the silence: then arose a cry,
And some ran forward, some stept staggering back,
  Covering their faces, and *one* wished to die.

For there she lay, who should have been a bride,
  Calm on her lover's breast, all pure and dead;
And fatefully the day shone, and a tide
  Of wind rolled coldly, moaning woe o'erhead.

Thus in my dream the tides of life turned back,
  Seeking past shores; till the pale soul stood still,
Sun-like, above the dead, through the wild rack
  · Of doubting anger pondering human ill.

Then said I, slowly turning eager eyes
  Upon those visionary lips that smiled in prayer,
"O that thou would'st reveal, since thou art wise,
  Passed beyond death, thus breathing larger air,

What said the Judge, the Infinite Holiness,
   When sudden, like a dove driven from its nest,
Broke on His calm this earthly wretchedness,
   Bearing its blood-stain, flame-wise on the breast!"

For we amid our tangled brake of life
   Grope heavily, knowing little, lost among
The mazes of the will; yet all our strife
   We think ends not alone in power of wrong.

Somewhere we trust the widening path shall slope
   Up to those quiet lawns, where evermore
The clear day shines, and windless isles of hope
   Sleep on below, beyond a waveless shore.

Somewhere, sometime, we think the dissonance
   Of all our pain shall pass into that psalm
Wherein God blends all chords, even ignorance
   To perfect music, last to perfect calm.

But she no answer made; but stood and prayed
   All silently with smiles upon her mouth,
And through the voids of sleep the wide seas made
   A murmurous music dying in the south.

Then just as all the loosened threads of sense
  Knitted themselves to action, and my dream
Waned like a star when darkness swoons immense
  Before the morn, there fell a subtle gleam

That touched her with a glory, and I heard
  Her speak the answer; but though much I strove
To catch the meaning yet but one faint word
  Reached me across the abyss, that *God was love.*

Whereat, when she had said, a sudden mist
  Snatched her away; and on the highest hill
I saw the Day ride, robed in amethyst,
  And waking, thanked my God my doubt was still.

A SERMON BY OLIVER CROMWELL.

.INTO the city at dawn of day,
Oliver Cromwell, stern and gray,

Rode at the head of his saints, and said :
" This city must find me money and bread."

A grim smile ran like a flash of light
Down the ragged lines in their famished plight,

And they thought of the wilderness way the Lord
Had led them, and joyed at Oliver's word.

Straight up the silent streets they prest
Round-head musketeers four-a-breast;

But the shops were empty, the people gone,
And for bread they had left them streets of stone

Then Oliver's shaggy brows grew black,
And the cloud of his anger did not slack

To see at the great Cathedral gate
The Mayor in his purple robes of state,

Plump with three sumptuous feasts a day,
Like a Pharisee going up to pray.

" Halt !" he called, and he stopped before
The beautiful temple's open door.

He looked to his right, and saw the van
Of his host, with faces scarred and wan.

He looked to his left, and saw the hoard
Of wealth in the temple of the Lord.

Twelve silver statues, six in a row,
Stood in the sunlight's softened glow;

And the quiet of God was in the place,
And the smile of God on each lifted face.

But Oliver looked on his men again,
And saw in their eyes the hunger-pain.

And straightway called to the trembling Mayor,
" What silver statues do you keep there ?"

Closer the Roundheads pressed, then stood
Still as a windless sea or wood.

Far above in the morning air
The gentle bells were full of prayer.

Then the Mayor answered, trembling much,
" The kingdom hath not twelve others such :

" John with Psalter, and Simon with sword,
The twelve Apostles of our Lord."

Oliver's gray eyes flashed beneath
His brows, like a sword pluckt from its sheath.

And he said, " My men, God hears our prayer,
Let us teach a lesson to Mr. Mayor.

" Apostles of silver I never heard
Could comfort the sick, or preach the Word.

" They must be tired of service and psalm,
Of indolent peace, or impotent calm.

" Kindle a fire, and drag them down ;
An idle saint is not worth a crown,

" But put to the uses of human need,
A saint is God's servant in truth and deed."

And then he added in kindlier mood,
" A saint should go about doing good ;

" These gentlemen coined into money will make
The world somewhat happier for their sake ;

" And so will perform, by deed if not lip,
The duties of their Apostleship."

8

COMPENSATIONS.

I SAW beside a sullen pool
   A bitter spirit brood,
Deep wrong was his, and loneliness,
   And doubt-infected blood.

The place was waste, and black, and scarred,
   As though some new-fall'n band
Of angels there had lit, and left   ·
   Their curse upon the land.

The bleak sky hung in leaden folds,
   And on a hill hard by
Three withered trees rose, like the three
   Crosses on Calvary.

At last along the moaning wind
   I heard a human cry,
And loud a human voice uprose
   Unto the leaden sky.

"O Thou, whose world men say this is !
 Hadst Thou been good or just,
Thou would'st have found some better sport
 Than building men of dust,

"Thou wouldst have paused, and feared per-
 chance
 The monster thing that leapt
Between Thy feet, with front like Thine,
 But heart where devils slept.

" Some other element Thou might'st
 Have found to clothe Thy plan,
Not river-slime, and desert-dust,
 And christened these—a man !

" Thou findest fire to make Thy stars,
 And goldenly they shine,
And air to build an azure dome,
 And winds to rouse like wine ;

" At least consistent in itself
 Each lamp that lights the skies ;
But man consistent is alone
 In inconsistencies.

" Thou hidest fire within his heart,
    But weakness in his hands;
All things he fain would comprehend,
    Yet nothing understands.

" A mighty-shouldered Samson Thou
    Hast fashioned and designed;
But brazen chains rust on his feet,
    And lo! his eyes are blind.

" And therefore cursèd be the day
    That gives the man-child birth:
So said Thy servant, and so groans
    Half of the living earth !"

The voice died down, as dies the storm
    With mutterings of pain;
And over the hollow plain there swept
    The wind, and now the rain.

The ragged edges of the clouds
    Trailed through as waste a flat,
As when the Flood began to ebb
    Beneath Mount Ararat.

The wind cried in each dismal tree,
  Each with its arms thrown wide,
As once around the Crosses three
  When Jesus Christ had died.

Again the voice said bitterly :
  " The worm within the sod
In character far more than man
  Betrays the hand of God.

" It works its slow way in the dark
  With curious certainty ;
Though it be blind, at least 'tis clear
  'Twas never meant to see.

" In man some faded line of grace
  We find, and call divine ;
And thus acknowledge he must be
  At best a spoiled design.

" Better to be a perfect thing,
  Though poor and low in plan,
Than this base birth of impotence,
  This hybrid, called a man !

‘ Each chord of sense snapped off in shame,
  Just where it touched the stars,
Each eagle-flight of nobleness
  Crushed back by prison-bars :

“ The brute's gross heart of flesh, and more,
  The spark of nether fire
Left in the soul to fructify,
  And scorch the high desire.

“ God's beauty, like the beauty left
  Within a harlot's face ;
Through all the putrid work of shame
  The gleam of former grace.

“ Ah, marvellous indeed to dream
  That this thing scales the sky !
What marvel that he lusts and lies,
  Himself the living lie ?”

The voice died down : and now the storm
  In milder gusts did blow.
The very wind was sad to see
  That solitary woe.

A gleaming light shot forth, and struck
   Upon the central tree
Of those three cross-like trees that crowned
   That dismal Calvary.

And in the white wan light it swayed,
   And forward leant, as though
It bore a Body, stained with blood,
   And white and dead with woe.

The voice again began in grief :
   " At least the plan were just,
That there should be no difference
   In creatures made of dust.

" Yet one within the golden walls
   Of comfort lies secure,
And hoarding sunlight of content,
   Lives scornful of the poor.

" But others live laborious days,
   And bend with dogged brow
Of dumb deep patience o'er their task,
   As cattle at the plough.

" And one walks through the yellow meads,
    And hears the birds at prayer,
And sings with them for very joy,
    And with as little care.

" While in the desert wander some,
    By palm and rock unscreened ;
Athirst for God, yet fed with husks
    And tempted by the fiend.

" If beast-like be the human heart,
    Better it were all brute,
Than like a tree, sun-topped in bough,
    But clay-bound in the root.

" Or since a certain likeness holds
    The million-featured race,
A common type that moulds the foot,
    And shapes the human face ;

" Let soul to soul be fashioned too,
    That one no longer be
The martyr to a thousand fools,
    Not less in will than he.

" Perchance we then could acquiesce
    In common sloth or sleep,
And lose the bitterness of tears,
    Remembering all men weep.

" O, curse of fate that bares the back
    Of one beneath the whip,
And lets the thousand pass to death
    With an unwhitened lip ;

" That bids him, as in mockery
    Survey the soul within,
And take his comfort that he bleeds
    For holiness, not sin !"

The voice died down, the light broke forth,
    And on the central tree
There clearly hung a dying man,
    Who moved in misery.

Forlorn the face drooped, ringed around
    With an acanthus wreath ;
The steady drops of blood fell down
    And soaked the turf beneath.

The blue broad bruise of scourge and blow
  Lay deep on side and limb ;
Alone within the dying eyes
  Shone life pain could not dim.

And straightway like an organ's pomp
  Subdued to tenderest breath,
Another Voice arose, and filled
  That desolate plain of death.

" Hast thou forgotten Who it was
  That set thy feet upright,
And made thee conscious of the Light
  That lives within the light ?

" Thou enviest the gross content
  Of bird, and beast, and worm :
Art thou so certain of the truth
  Of this thou dost affirm ?

" Within soft eyes of laden beasts
  Hast thou perceived no woe ?
Perchance their pain is greater far
  Than men who make it know.

" Ignoble thou!   The spark of God
　Within thy manhood leaps,
And fires the heap of dross whereon
　Thy scorpion-baseness sleeps.

" And thou would'st stamp the cleansing fire
　Out wholly, spark by spark,
And ask for leave to sleep again
　Within thy noisome dark.

" Thou would'st that man were wholly beast,
　Or wholly angel made ;
Brute blackness, with no touch of light,
　On sunlight without shade.

" And were it so, would aught be gained
　Of wisdom in the plan?
If God gave all things at the birth
　What task were left for man ?

" God's seasons climb on shining stairs,
　And starting in the bleak
White waste, stand crowned with light at last
　On Summer's highest peak.

" God's creatures, be they bird or beast,
　　Fight upward to their life,
And snatch their breathing time at last
　　In strength that comes of strife.

" Shall it be strange that man shall rise
　　On steps that slip with blood,
Up higher, to the strength, the light,
　　The summer of his God ?

" Stand up, O man, and bear thy lot :
　　'Tis neither more nor worse
Than all have borne ; and blessing shines
　　Far off, beyond the curse.

" Or if within thy darkened brain
　　Again the question strives,
' With me abides the woe, not so
　　It clings to other lives.'

" Consider, whether in the days
　　That dawn there shall not be
Some compensation, some reward,
　　Not otherwise for thee.

" In highest skies, on winds of calm,
  Within the still, wide light,
Those walk who fought their way to God
  Out of the deepest night.

" Far, far beneath, at best in some
  Restricted Paradise,
They lift their eyes, whom thou to-day
  Art envying as the wise.

" Or lastly, I, the world's long Vision,
  More God, not less by pain,
May somewhat teach : my crown is Thorn,
  I live by being slain."

The Voice died down, and clearly now
  The full sun shone between
The drifted clouds ; and lo ! the tree
  That seemed a cross was green.

The hollow waste caught eager life,
  The sudden lark soared up ;
The lonely pool so gleamed, it seemed
  Gold wine in emerald cup.

And all the vision passed away ;
The bitter spirit's cry
I heard no more ; the lark alone
Was singing in the sky.

FAREWELL.

METHOUGHT the world was changed. Ah! very
    drear
  The light that shone! Ah! sad the winds that
    blew!
Yet never day awoke so bright and clear;
Only I could not see the light, nor hear
  The song of any bird that flew.

I walked the lonely house with troubled eyes
  Of parting recognition; all was still.
The household pets looked up in meek surprise,
To feel my tears drop; and that strange sunrise
  Ghost-like stole on, all pale and chill.

Farewell! Farewell! O how from room to room
  That quivering chord swept like a dying sigh!
O silent house! O sunlight turned to gloom!
O wounded life that bled away thy bloom!
  Was not that anguish what it is to die?

A DIRGE OF MEMORY.

I.

ALL life stands still : the daisies grow
   Above thy icy bosom,
No more for thee the rose shall blow,
   Nor shall the violet blossom.
     And the lilies sweet
     About thy feet
Shall weep, and bend, and sicken :
     But never again·
     The summer strain
Of lark and linnet, through wood and plain,
   Thy quiet heart shall quicken.

II.

Thy lips are dust, thy golden hair
   With earthly clods is tangled ;
To me each sound of earth, once fair,
   Is like sweet music jangled.

Thy heart is dust, thy soul with God
  Hears no dear earth-names spoken;
In my heart flows the red, red blood,
  And yet my heart is broken.

JUNE IN LONDON.

THE roar of the streets at their loudest
   Rises and falls like a tune :
Mid-day in the heart of London,
   Midway in the month of June.

I cover my eyes a moment,
   To shut out the blinding glare,
And see in the dark a mirage
   Built out of golden air.

Green fields and blossoming orchards,
   And woods where the thrushes sing :
And white, through the chestnut's shadow,
   Farm-houses glistening.

And blue, at the end of the valley,
   I see the ocean gleam,
And a voice like the falling of water
   Speaks to me through my dream.

It calls, and it bids me follow :
  And do not the worn nerves thrill
At the vision of those green pastures,
  And waters running still ?

But I dare not move or follow,
  For out of the quivering heat
Another vision arises,
  And darkens at my feet.

White faces worn with the fever
  That crouches evermore
In the court and alley, and seizes
  The poor man at his door,

Float up in my vision and call me,
  And cry, " If Christ were here,
He had not left us to perish
  In the fever-heat of the year."

God knows how I yearn for the mountains,
  And the river that runs between !
Ah, well ! I can wait—and the pastures
  Of heaven are always green.

A SONG OF LIFE.

HEAVEN is over and round us, dust and corruption
    beneath,
The beating of wings stirs in us, like to the pulsings
    of breath,
As though in the heart our angel fluttered 'twixt
    life and death,
       And the æons of years roll on.

The æons of years roll on, and the earth is ever the
    same,
And man like a breath is lost in whirlwinds of
    sorrow and shame,
And knoweth not whither he goeth, and wondereth
    whence he came,
       And while he wonders is gone.

Like a bird's note heard in the hush betwixt the
    thunder and rain,
Between the rush of the ages he utters his cry of
    pain,
And the infinite storm rolls on across the infinite
    main,
       And who knoweth what he said?

And the planets wheel down their grooves, and the
    day breaks still and fair,
Lighting his sightless eyes with a cold and sickly
    glare,
And the west wind stirs and sings within the silk
    of his hair,
       And knoweth not he is dead.

His brother shall pass this way, and whistle along
    his path,
Not knowing what secret dread the depth of the
    forest hath,
And the grass growing round his face fears not the
    presence of death,
       And who shall make for him moan?

And the thrush upon his forehead shall merrily
    perch and sing,
But not an inch shall he stir, however her song shall
    ring,
And so shall he lie and rot: and ever on eagle
    wing
        The æons of years roll on.

Yet he measured perchance the breadth of the
    heavens with cunning brain,
And counted the stars by night, and gazed on the
    purple pain
Of the travailling day, and sought in treasures of
    Wisdom gain,
        And was it but vainly done?

Or rather shall we not think that greater he needs
    must be
Who crosses the sea of life, than ever can be the
    sea
That is his servant; and so the dead in his
    majesty
        Is more than the stars and sun.

Heaven is over and round us, dust and corruption
    beneath,
And all the years of our life like the sob of an
    infant's breath,
Who sleeps on the breast of his nurse : and the
    blinding wheels of death
        Crush us down into the sod.

So we sob out our life, and we fall into quiet and
    dust ;
And yet we fancy at times in the joy of our infant
    trust
We may wake when the fever is past, like a little
    child sleep-flusht,
        And know that our nurse was God.

Infinite unto the infinite, thus is the life of
    man.
Who cares whether it be of larger or lesser
    span ?
He dwelt in the heart of God before the world
    began,
        And thither returns again.

Like a lightning flash he burns across the infinite
    sky,
And writes his crooked story of life that never can
    die,
And vanishes into the cloud that covers the pitying
    eye
        Of Him who watcheth his pain.

The thought of his God is he, and God is his end
    and source,
For the awful heavens hold not so all-divine a force;
'And what though the suns of glory flash through
    an endless course,'
        And the æons of years roll on,

Yet crush they not his spirit, which flutters a
    prisoned wing
Within its shell, until Death brings sudden quicken-
    ing;
Then up through the deep it flieth, and in God's
    heart shall sing
        When the heavens are burned and gone.

FLOWER-FACES.

THERE be fair violet lives that bloom unseen
In dewy shade, unvext by any care ;
And they who live them wear the flower-like face
Of simple pureness, which amid the crowd
Of haggard brows strikes like a sweet perfume
Upon the jaded sense. God covers them,
Maybe, beneath the shadow of His wing,
That they may sweeten all His dark for Him,
And from their secret place waft airs of calm
Upon His troubled worlds. Sometimes they are
The holy sisters, who with wakeful eyes
Watch by the sick in dreary hospitals,
Close to the battlefield. Sometimes I see
The face gleam out beneath a Quaker hood,
More lily-like than violet, silver-haired,
With exquisite eyes of silent blessedness ;
And sometimes they be wives whose wedded love
Is fortunate, who always hear the mirth

Of children's voices like a babbling brook
Follow them through the dusty ways of life.
And sometimes 'tis a fair young rustic face,
Peach-shaded with the purity of health ;
And she, the Mother of the Christ, looked thus,
But sadder, with the holy stain of tears
Upon her bloom like rain on bursting buds.
But whensoe'er I see the liquid eyes
And smiling innocence, I think of flowers
That grow upon a mossy bank in spring,
When larks are singing in the windy skies,
And all my spirit rises up in praise
Because God's world holds in its wrecked design,
His image still, who made it very good.

THE ISLE OF LIFE.

IN the dawn of the world there rose
From the wells of the still gray seas
The mystic islands of life,
Where the day was never full day,
   And the night was never full night,
But a low sun shone alway,
   And it was not dark nor light.

And the children of men grew up,
And the daughters of men were fair,
And the sons of men were strong ;
And they built their cities and homes,
And the noise of man's various life
Was mixed with the winds and seas.
But the eyes of the men were sad,
And the children's laughter chilled :
For the strong man saw his wife
Worn down with the fires of pain,
And wasted with work and care :

And many suns waxed and waned,
But of labour there was no end.

And the child saw old men grouped
In the nooks of the market-place,
And they chattered with age and cold,
And wearied, but did not die.
Like the ghostly shadows of life
They moved, with their blinded eyes,
And hands so twisted with pain,
They looked like the hideous knots
At the roots of a witch's tree ;
And their palsied faces shook,
And their dwindled limbs were like
The boughs when the leaves are gone,
Which the children shuddered to see,
And fled with fear at their hearts,
Or clung at the father's knee,
Aghast at the vision of age.
For at last the cities were ful
Of dreadful faces and forms,
That moved like walking decay
Which cries to be covered up :
And they haunted the fancies of men,
Till the strongest turned, and groaned—
For the island had no graves.

And sickness dwelt in the land,
And no doors bore the sign
The angel knew and obeyed.
For in every house there writhed
Some huddled body, drawn up
By the cords of its agony
Out of human form or shape;
And parched delirious lips
Babbled obscenest things,
A shame and a woe to hear,
As though some devil within
Stirred in the native mud
Out of which man was made,
Defiling the temple of thought.
And the pestilence passed and left
The land full of wasted forms,
And idiot lips that brawled,
And hollow-eyed crowds that moaned
With the weight of their hopelessness,
And the dull endurance of pain.

And the golden hair grew gray,
And the strong man, old and pinched,
Sat now with his shivering hands
Stretched out by the fire, and wept.

And variance dwelt between
All hearts, and the anger of doubt
Gnawed at the roots of love ;
Or in deep oblivious age,
Full of selfish fretting and care,
Men sunk, and they moved like ghosts
Whose lips are sealed in dismay.
For the weary course of the years
Brought nothing new, nor sweet ;
And the moan of the still gray sea,
And the light of dim low day,
Became at the last to all
The voice of a ceaseless woe,
And the symbol of their despair.

Then at last a solemn barge,
Full of fluting choristers,
And bearing a maiden dead,
Drew near, by a wandering chance,
And paused at the mystic shore.
And out of each place in the land
The wasted people flocked,
And crowded about the bier,
And looked on the face of the dead
In its beautiful frozen calm,

Till at last the multitude
Joined in one mighty cry,
As the cry of a single man,
" O, that we, too, were dead !"
And the fluting choristers
Looked with eyes of amaze,
And said, " Can this be life,
And can it be death is sweet ?
For we have shuddered to see
This creeping eclipse called death,
 And have trembled to touch the dead ;
And lo ! here is no death,
But the land of a deathless life,
Which has haunted the visions of men,
And its life is worse than death,
And its immortality
A burden too heavy to bear,
And its people cry aloud
That the gods will let them die !"

Then there spoke from the midst of them all
The father, who erstwhile bowed
And wept by the maiden's lips,
And moaned, but never had moved :

"Yonder, beyond the seas,
Are the isles of life and death,
Where the day is the birth of night,
And the sea is vext by storms,
And the strong man dies in his prime,
And the bride on her marriage-morn,
And the child in his mother's arms,
And the land is full of graves.
If ye seek it, lo ! there it lies,
Where the northern heavens shine,
And the starry Wain lies low."
Then along the crowded shore
There murmured a cry of hope,
And the ghastly multitude
Thronged to the edge of the sea,
And with boats and rafts put forth,
And followed the barge of the dead,
With its fluting choristers,
Till at last through the mist and foam
They saw the land grow clear,
And heard through the stormy seas
The tolling of many bells,
And they touched the shore, and died.

A CHILD'S PORTRAIT.

HER face is hushed in perfect calm,
  Her lips half-open hint the psalm
The angels sing, who wear God's palm :
  And in her eyes a liquid light,
With somewhat of a starry sheen,
  Comes welling upward from the white
And vestal soul that throbs within.

A golden tangle is her hair
  That holds the sunlight in its snare ;
And one pure lily she doth wear
  In her white robe : and she doth seem
A flower-like creature, who will fade
  If suns strike down too rude a beam,
Or winds blow roughly on her shade.

The golden ladders of the Dawn
　　Meet at her feet, where on the lawn
She stands, in tender thought withdrawn:
　　And little wonder would it be,
If on those slanting stairs she trod,
　　And with one farewell smile toward me,
Were caught into the smile of God.

LIFE WITH LOVE.

I.

UPWARD shot the sun
  Above the level brim
Of the hollow cup-like world ;
  And the golden light, like wine,
In a cataract was hurled,
  And bubbled around the brim
Of the beautiful broad world,
  Which hung in the hyaline
Like a chalice of leaping light,
Upheld by the hands of night.

II.

Upward shot the sun
  Above the clouded rim
Of my hollow thirsting soul ;
  And the foaming light of love
Filled life's crystal bowl,

And melted the vapours dim
That hung about my soul :
And far in the feast above
I saw the Hand that poured,
And knew that it was the Lord !

LIFE WITHOUT LOVE.

I.

DOWNWARD fell the sun
  Behind the world's red rim,
Like another world on fire ;
  And a blood-red splendour burst,
Like the flame's last leap, when spire
  ' And steeple fall : and dim
The earth lay, and the fire
  Died down ; and there accurst,
And black and barren lay
The world once bright with day.

II.

Downward fell the sun
  Behind the new year's rim,
Like a heart shot through with pain,
  Which throbs forth blood, and then
Lies black, and quiet, and slain.

And my soul waxed cold and dim
Like a world aswoon with pain,
And fearing help of men ;
And the darkness spread and spread,
Till I knew my soul was dead.

THE LAST RIDE OF THE
SHEIK ABDULLAH.

INTO the desert, into the desert
　　All alone I ride,
At last the clamour of tongues is still,
The fever of living, the strife of will,
The doors of the old sick life flung wide
　　Let me out, and thus I ride.

I fight no longer for standing-room,
Tricked by folly and tripped by doom,
Strive no longer to find life's rule,
Or win the prizes in race or school.
How dieth the wise man? As the fool!
　　And into the desert I ride.

Under my feet the wide world slides,
Over my head one still star glides,
It is earth that slides back like a tide,
And heaven comes rushing up as I ride,
　　As all alone I ride.

Silent as never was city or sea,
Empty of man, or house or tree,
   The desert lies round me as I ride:
The blue sky shuts down everywhere
Close on the earth, the quivering air
Parts like a flame that winds divide,
   And closes behind me as I ride.

Ah, joy of Freedom! Let me ride
Forever and ever, on, still on,
Till all the stars that flickered and shone
Have fallen behind me, one by one,
Till I touch the blue steep wall of air,
And suddenly draw rein at God's stair,
Coming on heaven unaware,
   As over the desert I ride.

Tamed and caged for many a day
In the world's market hot and gray,
I have danced to pipes that wealth can play.
I have won great gold—to fling it away;
And knowledge—to pluck it by its root;
And pleasure—to crush its hollow fruit:
Now, into the desert all alone,
I ride at peace, for all are gone.

I shall ride right on to God's feet,
For my heart is strong, my camel fleet :
I shall ride on, and never stop
Till close at His palace stair I drop.
The earth slides under me like a tide,
My life runs out of me as I ride,
   I die as I ride, I ride and die,
   I ride right on to eternity.
How dieth the wise man ?   As the fool !
What matters life's living? This is death's rule!
And so I ride, in one last burst
Of glorious freedom quenching thirst
And yearnings crushed in the years accurst
Which, barren as sand, behind me lie :
   I die as I ride : I ride and die.

TO A LITTLE CHILD.

DEAR child, with eyes of heaven's stain
  And face like fair flowers blowing,
It fills me with a sense of pain
  To see how fast thou'rt growing.

But yesterday heaven's crystal door
  Unclosed, and we received thee ;
To-morrow thou wilt find how poor
  The world that has deceived thee.

Already with such serious eyes
  Thou look'st between thy kisses,
I feel that thou art growing wise,
  Too wise for childhood's blisses.

I think of Jesus full of glee
  Within the sunlit meadows,
And Mary with sad eyes that see
  Far off the Cross's shadows.

And I could almost bow and pray,
"O Lord, if this Thy will is,
Let this sweet child forever play
Amid sweet Nazareth's lilies!"

That thou must leave this happy plain,
To life's steep Calvary going!
It fills me with a sense of pain
To see how fast thou'rt growing.

THE RIVER.

SING, little stream, in thy pebbly bed,
   While I drowsily dream and listen,
Watching the eddies that bubble and swirl,
   And the bubbles that break and glisten.
And the thrush in the tree that is bending o'er thee
   Sees his shadow that wavers and quivers,
And sings a fresh solo; and thou in thy glee
   Art his chorus, O sweetest of rivers!
Rippling and singing away to the sea,
Chorus for all who joyful can be,
   Art thou, O sweetest of rivers!

Ah! that my life ran ever in song
   Over years that but broke it in sweetness,
With ripple and murmur, and eddy and pause,
   Till it lost the sense of its fleetness;

And only made music of word and of deed
  To the song of the soul, who sits singing,
A thrush in the bower of the heart, till the need
  Of death comes, and quiets the singing.
O river! clear river, from lands far away,
See what a sweet thought to a singer to-day
  Thy rippling and bubbling is bringing!

SONG FOR A GONDOLA.

Lieder Ohne Worte, 6.

I.

CHANTING, chanting, chanting,
Not loudly but with measured note,
While on the tideless sea we float
Between the houses grand and tall,
　And moonbeams bright and slanting.
Ah! see how deep the shadows fall
By yonder prison's gloomy wall;
And now we flash into the light
Through waves of silvery fire; and bright
Before us spreads the open sea
Running into Eternity;
And on we glide, and ever we
　Are chanting, softly chanting.

II.

Slow and solemn chant we all,
In requiem notes that rise and fall,
While like a swan the gondola
    All dark and dying glides along,
And we her soul and death-song are.
    Was ever song so clear and brave
Sung to the trembling stars, each star
    Itself a chord in God's great song?
        Dying, dying, dying,
        Black on the wave
    The shadow of our swan is lying.
And flutters away toward her grave.

III.

    No more! No more!
The gentle sea is never still;
    The ripples splash on stair and shore,
        But ye are quiet all,
And the swan lies floating, floating still,
    Through water-shadows that rise and fall,
And the moonlit air is chill.

O Gondolier, awake, awake !
But never a single word he spake,
And the snowy moonlight, flake by flake
Fell on his face and lips all still.
    Floating, floating, floating,
By palace and marble stair no more,
  But ever to music soft and low,
  In dream or trance, I know not how,
I touch the mystic further shore.

AT PARTING.

" Is it all over, then ?"
O dare you ask me, when too well you know
The deed that parts us ?   Must I once more go
Over the story of our blame to show
How utterly the silver cord is loosed,
How the great golden bowl, so long misused,
Lies broken, and the mourners wail about
    My heart ?   O when
Did love bend to the withering wind of doubt,
    And rise, and bloom again ?

II.

This even must I say,
Since still you vex the question with reply,
Love has no resurrection, though you try
All means to wake the slain face and closed eye.

Who tries to call the sun back ?   Every bird
Reads the inevitable, undeterred
By the red glow the sunset simulates ;
    And so straightway
Wails his last flute-note, and in silence waits
    The hush.of murdered day.

III.

    The sere leaves fall like rain ;
Bend thou the bough, but can'st thou put back one,
That it shall grow, and drink the wind and sun ?
There are things done which cannot be undone.
Love's is the seamless raiment of the soul,
And thou would'st patch its rents.   But never whole
And white again can be the robe divine,
    Its God being slain.
Far in the sky Love's flying feet still shine,
    And we—we bear our pain.

IV.

    Think not I love to wound.
Poor child ! what know you of the inner mind
Of love's divinest depths?   Were it not blind
To veil the fatal fault ? .Shook by the wind,

You stand here like a lily, pale with pain,
And for thy love God knows my heart is fain!
But well I know 'tis best to part, even though
  Hope's night close round,
Rather than with divided hearts to go
  Till both rest underground.

V.

O leave me, leave me, sweet!
Stained howsoe'er with fault, still dear to me.
To-night you'll weep ; to-morrow I foresee
Thy pain will ebb, as ebbs the troubled sea,
And then the bright thin smile will dawn again.
But even as men remember some sweet strain
Of song through life, and hear even as they die
  Its rhythmic beat,
So shall I hear thee, God's world tremblingly
  Echoing to thy feet.

VI.

Go now : one timorous
Brief moment thus we kiss. Let us not part
As those who wrest the petty actor's art,
We, who have rested child-like heart on heart.

Go thou, and God be with thee in thy tears!
Who knows what wisdom waits thee with the years?
Perhaps—who knows?—beyond this world's thick
    air,
     Again, not thus,
We yet may meet. Wait for me there—even there.
    God keep and pity us!

THEN AND NOW.

THROUGH months of quiet dawn and eve
   I watched the shadows on the hill,
The light that was so loath to leave   -
   The saffron west ; and all too still,
Too void of life that sweet world seemed,
Of London's louder world I dreamed,
     So dull that seemed,
     So deathly still !

In London's louder world I dwell
   And watch the lurid smoke-cloud drift;
I watch, and ask, Ah ! was it well
   For this gray sky which has no rift
To barter that sweet calm of old,
Those days that broke and set in gold,
     That life of old,
     Ah ! was it well ?

In London's louder world no brooks
   Go singing unseen through the shade ;
Immured in streets, I write in books
   The songs that once leapt ready-made
To fit the music which I heard
Babble in brook, and break in bird.
     O blessed shade !
     O sweet-voiced bird !

MY HEART.

I.

MY heart sings like a cloistered nun,
  My heart sings like a hidden bird ;
Through tangled roofs of green, the sun
Has dropped a golden patch of light,
  And here my heart sits like a bird
  Whose little brain with joy is stirred,
Because the great world is so bright.

II.

My heart sings like a cloistered nun,
  Who dreams of that sweet world foregone
Where life's bright dream itself begun ;
At last the sunlight makes her weep
  With thoughts of all that is foregone,
  The lover's kiss, and love's dear tone,
The mother-joy, divine and deep.

III.

My heart sings all alone, alone,
   And no one hears the song she sings!
If on the cloister's barren stone
The world's hard foot is heard, my heart
   Is like a bird, who, while she sings
   Flutters her golden frightened wings,
And drops, as stricken by a dart.

MORNING DREAMS.

I ROUSE, and see a golden light
  Strike through the blinds, and on the wall
It trembles like a fire, with bright
  Clear subtle threads that rise and fall :
  No sound is in the street at all,
And thus I know for one brief space
The world lies open to God's face.

I sleep again : I seem to sink
  In seas of hazy light ; I hear
Bright waves that break upon the brink
Of far-off shores ; and now again
  The dim confusion grows more clear,
And in my dream I wake and think.

I see great fields of ripened grain,
The lark's song thrills into my brain.
I see great ships upon the sea,
And waves that run on endlessly.
I see great cities lying fair,
Asleep within this golden air.
And far on Indian plains I see
The sun sink on his way to me.
And one deep music everywhere
   Beats up and down, and shakes the light
Like a vast flail, and this must be
The million million hearts that beat
To one slow time through cold and heat,
   Or my own heart—I know not quite.

I rouse, I sleep, I dream once more :
   A strange sense haunts my being now,
That I have seen this place before,
   This house, this dew-dripped neat hedge-row
This sun, just poised above the bend
   Of yon blue hill, and this brook's flow
Runs through my brain world without end.
God bless you !   Ah, what lips were those ?
   The light folds like a door, and lo !
For just one moment—how, who knows ?

A girl-form steps down living stairs
Of gold, and gliding unawares,
   Has kissed me on the brow.   Ah, so
   She kissed me in days long ago !
I wake, and on the chamber-wall
The threads of fire still rise and fall.

A BOOK OF DAYS.

THE LAST SPRING.

I.

So beautiful this year the spring hath been,
    That on these early morns, when I have stood
Above the valley's cup-like sea of green,
    And watched the light shift, something moved
        my blood
To exquisite sadness, and my heart has said,
    " Is this the last spring that shall ever be ?
And like a dying man, raised on his bed,
    Whose face a moment shines majestically
With an angelic youth, does the strong earth
    Display her inmost beauty, knowing well
How mortal weakness follows such a birth?
    Next year—the judgment thunder, deeps of hell,
The infinite wail of scorched and cursèd lips !
This year—the calm air where the swallow dips.

II.

If this were so, even then could I be strong
  In hope, and fear not.   Dark, as in a glass,
I see the phantom-vision move along,
  Smitten of God, and stricken down as grass.
Then all lies dead : the fire-sown wastes smoke on
  A little while : the dreadful trumpets stilled
Leave a world without sound, or word, or moan,
  A Desolation, unnamed and untilled.
But is this more, or worse, than what hath been ?
  What if it burn and blacken, year by year,
Through awful æons ? Yet shall it be green
  When the full time is come; and light more clear
And meads more sweet, and birds more bright of
    wing
Shall fill the new heavens and new earth with
    spring.

III.

Or last I thought, how likelier shall it be
This sadness prophesies not earth's last spring,
  But simply earth's last spring that buds for me
A moment's space I heard no thrushes sing,

I marked no tangled lights of cloud and sun,
But saw in vision a house stand with drawn blinds,
  Wherein broods Silence o'er a silent one,
Whose pale cheeks quicken with no mild May
        winds,
Nor eyes fill with sweet tears.   Last night for him
  The fragrant silence throbbed, the nightingale
Sang him to sleep.   At last the light rose dim,
  And they who watched broke forth into a wail:
The silver cord was loosed at morn's first breath,
The golden bowl broke at the feet of Death.

A SYMBOL.

A LARK in a lurid sky
  Hung close at the lips of the thunder,
Singing his quiet evensong
  To the dark world lying under.

The gathering tempest burst
  With a roar of god-like anger,
Waking the King on his silken bed,
  And the Babe in his holy manger.

And then the sun broke forth
  On the fragrant fields of clover :
And the lark sang on in the naked sky,
  Like a Soul when death is over.

BIRTH AND DEATH.

Two visions the sun hath seen to-day
  Within the self-same shaded room,
And the world has passed from gold to grey,
  And the sunlight glided into gloom.

At morn a new-born infant's wail
  Ended the mothering pain and moan,
And the mother sighed with lips all pale,
  "Let me kiss it, my sweet, my own !"

At eve the infant's fretful cry
  Stirred the self-same shaded room,
But no lips answered with a sigh :
  The mother was dead within the gloom.

And so the song of Life runs on,
 Though singers pass, or singers come;
And endlessly the suns have shone,
 And the world rolled round from gold to
 gloom.

SUNRISE.

DAY treads the mountains, like a spirit drest
  In rayless raiment, and the morning star
    Glares through a sickly vapour deep and dun,
Yet lingering like a late and homeless guest.
  Then suddenly above the leaden bar
    Of envious clouds leaps the unprisoned sun.
O sing me, dearest love! some morning song
  To chaunt beside the cradle of the Day,
The sweet young Day, so pure from earthly wrong,
  Who rides within the sunlight's golden spray,
A burning babe, rocked on a tide of fire
  Yet unconsumed, being the child of God.
I faint, I languish, I can but aspire,
  And worship, kneeling on this dewy sod.

MORNING.

THE great world sleeps, the village at my feet
    Lies still as death; the sea of soundless air
Moves gently like the quiet breath most sweet
    Betwixt an infant's lips. I cannot dare
To speak in such a Temple. But behold
    Above the level mists a solemn streak
Of tender light, a shaft of glorious gold,
    And all disordered now the grey clouds break;
And there below me is the shepherd's fold,
    And far away the bright, blue, slumbering lake.
Alas! the scene charms not as heretofore,
    For I am thinking while the glory grows
    Of vanished faces, voices hushed, and those
Who here will wander with me nevermore.

EVENING.

OFT have I seen set in the glowing west
  One fair bold star of mild eternal beam,
  Fast anchored in the sunset's purple stream,
A shining splendour lapped in perfect rest.
And when behind the hill the burning crest
  Has waned, and darkened, till all light was gone,
  Fairer and fairer still that lone star shone,
Like a new sun in pallid glory drest.
  High in the drifting clouds I saw it gleam
Like a deserted prophet, near God's throne,
Who cries, "Of all thy prophets I alone
  Remain to serve Thee!" And I dreamed a
    dream
That thus our Milton stood amid the night,
Faithful, alone, Hope's bright and shining light.

STARLIGHT.

THE eternal stars, they are the founts of flame
    Where God hath trodden; round His mighty
      feet
They blossomed as He walked, and spelt His name
In living splendours, that all men might know
    What reverent fear from man towards Him is
      meet,
From whose deep heart the life of all doth flow.
Again they kindle through the gleaming skies,
    Venus, Orion, the sweet Pleiades,
Ranged like an army, with the endless blue
One banner o'er them. Still they set and rise,
    And evermore the wonder doth increase
With deeper knowledge. For I hold this true,
Who made the heavens doth heed a sparrow's fall,
And He who loveth one, He loveth all.

MIDNIGHT.

THIS is the place and hour to worship God,
   Whose dome of blue bends starry o'er my brow,
   Quivering on viewless pillars.　Day lies low,
And dies amid the drowsy flowers that nod
Like watchers round a bed ; the solemn spheres
   Roll onward, making music as they move
About the burning throne, and to my ears
   It is a chorus of perpetual love.
This is the hour, while all the world doth sleep,
   To breathe the wakeful sorrow, to arise
And set the heart free, and if it would weep,
   Weep forth its fulness.　For the eternal eyes
Can slumber not, and the eternal heart
Throbs nearest ours when hushed is town and mart

TWO DAYS.

SOME chord within is wrong.   The music is
   Confused through all my life.   But yesterday,
Such fresh keen thought I had, to live was bliss :
   To-day, the sullen skies hang low and gray,
No eagerness I feel to think or know,
   Nor hope for any future.   Mute I sit,
   And feel the impotence of baffled wit,
And Life troops past me in a mocking show,
Turning its worst side, its most shameful part,
   Which Hope keeps covered. Yet amid the gloom
Louder than yesterday I hear my heart
   Astir to face stern-browed the storm of doom.
Immortal music saddest is, and we
Unworthy God had life no agony.

GUIDANCE.

WHERE is the guiding star, and where the light ?
  The cloudy pillar screens and leads no more,
The shaft of fire no longer through the night
  Shoots solemn splendours, and we see not now
  What they saw, who looked up, and lo ! a door
In heaven opened, wherefrom fell the bright
  Full glory in its tranquillizing glow.
They slept and dreamed, and o'er the jasper wall
  God dropped His ladders, woven of the sun ;
They woke, and knew no evil should befall
  Their wandering feet, kept by the Wiser One.
Alas for us ! beneath blank heavens we sleep
And angels cannot climb a void so steep.

II.

Yet still the faith of ancient days is left,
  Albeit its dream and vision be withdrawn.
The rock within the desert hath its cleft
  Where meek content may dwell. There is a
    dawn
That brightens surely unto praying eyes,
  And breaks at last before the dying vision;
There is a mighty heart whose passionate cries
  Are birth - throes to the prophet's mightier
    mission.
I know not now, but, like those mariners
  Who dared forlorn the undiscovered seas,
I through uncharted wastes steer by the stars;
  And it shall be, at last, a vision of trees
Of life shall bound the deep, and I shall view
That Blessed Land, whereto all God's winds blew.

INSPIRATIONS.

SOMETIMES, I know not why, nor how, nor whence,
  A change comes over me, and then the task
  Of common life slips from me.   Would you ask
What power is this which bids the world go hence?
  Who knows?   I only feel a faint perfume
Steal through the rooms of life ; a saddened sense
Of something lost ; a music as of brooks
That babble to the sea ; pathetic looks
  Of closing eyes that in a darkened room
  Once dwelt on mine : I feel the general doom
Creep nearer, and with God I stand alone.
  O mystic sense of sudden quickening !
Hope's lark-song rings, or life's deep undertone
  Wails through my heart—and then I needs must
    sing.

A VISION OF DEATH.

I DREAMED a dream, whereat the healthy blood
  Through all my veins stood still. An awful
    Shade
  Steeped to the lips in glooms, with brow that
    made
Darkness yet darker, by my bed-side stood.
His face was like a white and flickering fire,   '
  Each instant changing; but the solemn eyes
  Were fixed as stars, shining in moonless skies,
Beyond the surge of tumult or desire.
The Shadow moved, and on his pallid brow
  An ebon crown gleamed; then, with bated
    breath
  I asked was this indeed the form of Death?
Like whispered music fell the answer, "No,
  'Twas God's own shadow falling on the child
  He lifted higher." Then I awoke, and smiled.

THE TRIUMPHANT SOUL.

DEEP in the roaring world there is a spot
  Of central calm ; the whirlwind's inmost soul
  Is peace. Swift to the horizon's goal
The eternal storm beats on ; but I move not,
Nor breath of danger stirs the slenderest hair ;
  For, poised within this calm, I see the world
Like a vast wheel that spins through humming air,
And Time, Life, Death, are sucked within its
    breath,
  And thrones and kingdoms like sere leaves are
    hurled
Down to its maelstrom, and its wind of death
'Sweeps the wide skies, and shakes the flaring suns,
So fast the wheel spins, and the glory runs.
O joy ! that thus amid the roar of things
Drawn down to death, man's soul stands calm and
    sings.

CREEDS AND CHRIST.

TO-DAY within an infamous house I stood
And saw a woman die.   Her black hair streamed
Around her sunken eyes, wherein there gleamed
Delirious light.   A priest stood over her,
And held the Cross : he saw a womanhood
Yet undestroyed by brutal days of shame,
And yearned within his faithful arms to bear
The lost sheep home to the Good Shepherd's care.
In that foul room all faces evil were,
Even the dying ; but as the woman drew
Nigh her last hour, some long-dulled memory leapt . . .
Like a stung nerve within her, and she prayed
In snatches of such prayer as once she knew
In the green village where a child she played,
And when with child-like folded hands she slept,
Lo ! all those evil faces watched and wept !

That day amid vext creeds my mind had striven
Till I had cried aloud in great despair,
Is there a Christ at all, or hell, or heaven ?
Did I not find the world's Good Shepherd there ?

WEALTH.

GREAT wealth is mine, well-earned and not soon
    lost,
  Treasure laid up in heaven, the mighty store
Of great men's greatest thoughts; such men as
    crossed
This world with nimble feet like spirits of light,
  Making a path where there was none before,
A chasm of light wedged in by blackest night.
  These long have led me; me, by pride of men
Shut out from palaces where monarchs sit,
  These, living in immortal vigour when
Empires and thrones red Ruin's fires have lit.
They make no stranger of me; with their wit
They cleanse my spirit, with their visions free
They build a heaven about me. Kings they be

Yet gird themselves to be my ministers,
And crowd my table with such dainty fare,
I smile to think how poor the millionnaire
   Who eats his sordid crust amid the curs
At Lazarus' gate, sunk lower even than they,
While I fare sumptuously every day.

A CURE FOR ENVY.

I STOOD within a rich man's house to-day,
  And saw his treasures with an envious heart.
  Among the costly rooms made rich with Art
At last I saw a room for children's play,
  Whereat a child's wide eyes might fill for joy,
So beautiful and perfect was the place.
  I asked the question, Had he then a boy,
Heir to his splendour, or did girlhood's grace
    Fill all his house with sweetness, and even here
      In this deep-windowed room did little ones
      Make glee from rising even to setting suns?
The answer came, no child had he at all,
  And for this reason is the great house drear:
  All that he hath of gold or art more dear
He fain would sacrifice, if there might fall
  Upon the perfumed air the babbled glee
Of one small child's clear voice. I cried, A
      Heaven!
  Thou gavest him the house, the child to me,
To me far more than to this man is given!

A DAYBREAK.

DEEP in the night of many things we spoke,
And as the hours wore, license loosed the tongue
To baser utterance. Friend, you had avowed
Your unbelief in love ; you straightway broke
The seal of shameful secrecy, and showed
How cruel and vile this bitter world could be,
And I remember with what scorn you flung
God's very name from you. We looked a space
Into each other's eyes, and then we rose,
Pushed back the table, flung the shutters wide,
And stepped into the air. The hour of three
Struck far away ; I turned, and on your face
Saw a still light reflected—'twas the morn.
The silent splendour flowed on like a tide
And filled the world, and I stood dumb and felt
How little is it that the wisest knows !

While we had given our hearts up to be torn
By doubt and passion, lo ! the God denied
Had worked this throbbing miracle of day.
I think you knew it.   Neither of us knelt,
And yet we felt the need and power to pray.

UNSATISFIED.

IT seemed such bitter anguish, yet it was
The thing that needs must be. Long years have
    hewn
A deep gulf, which we cannot cross, between
Our diverse lives. As in a wizard's glass,
I see twin shadows move, a lawn rose-strewn,
A winding-path upon a hillside green,
And that old day burns clear. I never should
Have kissed your lips, or having kissed them once,
Should then have left you. But not what we
    would,
But what we must, we do. Just for the nonce
I tarried with you, thinking I would turn
And fly before my passion gathered strength ;
But ever when I strove to breast that tide
I saw your eyes grow moist, your bosom yearn,
And though I felt my soul unsatisfied,

My senses loved you.   So it happed at length
We each beheld the other ; with clear scorn
You told me you had found me cold and base,
And I confessed my love like yours outworn.
We wronged each other.   Now your very face
Is a blurred portrait, and the shadows fall
So thick, and fold beneath their trailing hem
So much, I ask, "Did these things chance at all,
Or did I long since sleep, and dream of them?"

A STORM AT NIGHT.

THE wind roared round the lonely house last night
And held me sleepless.   I heard far beneath
The stifled thunder of the sea ; I heard
The wild shrill cry of some night-wandering bird
Pierce the loud uproar, and like passionate breath
Of great hosts lost in battle, wailed the storm,
And woke within me fearful thoughts of Death.
O Death ! I had conceived thee as a Form
Of stealthy murder, muffled in thick gloom,
And oft while looking in loved eyes I feared
Thy silent dagger ; but that loud storm cleared
Thy inner sky, and drew the sting of Doom.
Such infinite strength moved in that viewless wind
That I rejoiced.   For, if the worst thing come,
What is my worst, or I ?   Or what, I said,
Shall be the loss to Nature if my mind
Cease from its struggle, and my hands lie dead ?

Let me sink in this Infinite Whole ! Let me
Pass from these trivial torments forth to share
This vext loud tumult of the sea and air !
He who is fearless, he alone is Free.

THE FIRST-BORN.

THE bitterest and the gladdest hour it was !
I stood at the stair's foot and heard your cry
Ring through the house.   Upon the slanting glass
The setting sun made splendour, and I watched
Him sink with eyes which nothing saw.   Again,
A moment's space the chamber-door unlatched
Let out your moaning, and I bitterly
Bowed down and trembled at your voice of pain.
Eternity seemed crowded in that hour;   .
All thought and passion, faculty and power
Was quickened and intense; the veil of gross
And faulty apprehension was withdrawn,
And left the naked heaven of infinite things
Close to me, like a throbbing heart.   More close
I felt thy spirit, and I cried, " What now
If she be passing out on angel's wings ?"

Just then the sun sank to his other dawn,
And as his rim burned down in final glow,
I heard a new voice in the house, the cry
Of the new-born, whose kindling human light
Rose on our lives, and, please God, by-and-by
Shall shine far out athwart the world's dark night

DELIVERANCE.

In that sore hour around thy bed there stood
A silent guard of shadows, each equipped
With dart or arrow aimed against thy life.
Thy breath came slowly all that awful night;
Outside I heard the wind and earth at strife,
And on the window's ledge incessant dripped
The pitiless rain.   At last I left thy room,
And passing out, upon its threshold's edge
Who should I meet but Death!   A wan clear light
Fell from his fathomless eyes, his brow was gloom,
His rustling raiment seemed to sigh like sedge
When the salt marsh-winds wail and beat thereon.
He paused, he turned; and while I stood and wept,
Behold a crimson signal waved and shone
On the door's lintel, even such an one
As he obeyed in Egypt, and I knew
Death heard some higher summons, and withdrew :
When I returned, like a tired child you slept.

THE SLEEPING MOTHER.

How still the vast depths of this City's heart!
At last the ever-moaning tide of life
Is quiet, and, sweet mother, wearied thou
With the babe's wailing and its piteous strife,
Thou too, worn in love's toil, art tranquil now.
I watch thee, and I think how fair thou art
In this deep-lidded sleep; the uncoiled hair
Piled round the high clear brow, one white arm
    bare,
On which lies warm the little golden head
Wearier even than thine. And now I see
How sunk thine eyes are, and that forehead fair,
How fretted with faint lines unmerited
So early; and reproach lays hold of me,
That I have led thee from thy pastures green
To these steep slopes where we are bowed with
    care.

Yet if thou should'st awake and read my thought,
I know thine eyes would fill with light serene,
And thou would'st say, " This burden have I sought,
This service is a perfect liberty ;
This City of Love, whose pulse of life beats quick
With strenuous tasks, is it not better far
Than virgin pastures, where the air is thick
With golden languors and a dull content ?
Great joy hath woman when that time is spent,
And on her life there rises that new star
Which leads her feet where mother-raptures are."

THE LAST DAY.

THEN at the last, from her drawn dying lips
I saw her soul pass forth, as one might see
A bright flame quiver : then the great eclipse
Slow-settled on her brow, and all was dark.
So bowed was I with my sore agony,
That all my brain seemed numb, until a spark
Of new strange light, dropped from her soul's keen
    flame,
This trance or vision kindled in my mind.
I saw her Soul, far off and like a star,
Move in the dark deep heavens, and lo ! a wind
Blew bitterly, and sudden I became
A frail ghost caught within its upward whirl,
Until my feet trod heaven's outer bar.
Then once I turned, and saw this world lie far
Within her folded clouds, and once I turned
And saw the opening gates of God which burned
With clear deep light, as they were made of pearl.

And then I cried aloud, and lo! her soul
Drew near me on the wind a moment's space,
And smiled and vanished! And with that the
    whole
Dream like some shining bubble shook and broke:
With sound of my own weeping I awoke,
And lo! I wept upon her poor dead face.

LIFE'S CROWNING HOUR.

Now let me die! This one full hour of life
    Hath drained the heart dry. O this exquisite
      bliss,
This crowding of all thought, this urgent strife,
    This deep divine delirium—life is this!
In this consummate hour like one I stand
    Upon some topmost Alp: I see below
Great cities lie like scattered heaps of sand;
    I hear no sound save the air's quickened flow
When eagles stir their wings; my old life lies
    Like a forgotten dream; I am so close
To the blue doors of these immense still skies,
That but one finger's weight upon their latch
Will push them open, and God's flame will catch
    Me into its bright ecstasy; who knows?

THE REJOINDER.

Ah, love! do you remember how not long ago
   We strayed together by the summer shore,
What time I read you such sweet breaths of verse
   As stirred my heart perchance the night before ;
And though my rhymes were harsh, yet the deep
     sea
   Chiming between the lines took up their thought,
Like a great singer lifting a poor song
   Beyond itself to grandeur. When I sought
To say my verse was weak, limping behind
   My inner meaning, straightway you would lift
Your brimming eyes on mine, and falter forth
   Through tears and kisses praise beyond my gift ;
And so we watched the thickening stars in th' north,
And felt the deep heavens God's hand bent above :
     Do you remember, love ?

And love, do you remember how in those sweet
    days
  You called me your own poet, took my rhymes,
And put them in your bosom, with sweet guile :
  Kissing them slyly, kissing them many times ;
And bade me sing for you, and only you,
  Like a caged lark in dear captivity?
And you would sob applause, and cry, *Well done!*
  And give for fame a love that could not die.
And now beyond the privet-hedge of love
  Out to the open world my song has sounded,
And thou wilt say the world will share with thee
  Thy sacramental joy! O be not wounded!
I am thy poet still, and thou to me
The secret heaven wherein I sing and move,
    Remember this, sweet love!

THE END.

Elliot Stock, Paternoster Row, London.